THE
LADY IN WHITE

Moving across the room on tiptoe, I took a closer look at the photograph. It was apparently of Julia, taken when she was eighteen or twenty. She was dressed in her white bridal gown, the veil pulled back over her head, her long blonde hair falling casually about her shoulders. She was the image of the lady in white I had seen in the hallway.

The photograph mesmerized me. As I looked at it, I remembered her mad laughter and the terrifying scene of her standing above me, the knife raised high above her head. At that moment, the bedroom door swung slowly open and there, knife in hand, stood the real lady in white!

"You shouldn't have come back," she said in a pathetic, regretful whisper.

"I...I'm leaving," I stammered. "I'm leaving in the morning. My car..."

"It's too late," she said. "Too late, too late...."

DARK EDEN
is an original POCKET BOOK edition.

DARK EDEN

•

by
Barbara Kevern

PUBLISHED BY POCKET BOOKS NEW YORK

DARK EDEN

POCKET BOOK edition published June, 1973

This original POCKET BOOK edition is printed from
brand-new plates made from newly set, clear, easy-to-read type.
POCKET BOOK editions are published by POCKET BOOKS, a division of
Simon & Schuster, Inc., 630 Fifth Avenue, New York, N.Y. 10020.
Trademarks registered in the United States and other countries.

Standard Book Number: 671-77645-2.
Published by POCKET BOOKS, New York, and on the same day in
Canada by Simon & Schuster of Canada, Ltd., Richmond Hill,
Ontario.

Printed in the U.S.A   Cover art by Hector Garrido.

To Linda Shepherd
of Simi Valley
with love

Chapter One

It was raining when I brought the car to a stop near the entrance of Harmer House. I turned the engine off and waited for a lull in the downpour. The car was warm, and it was pleasant just sitting there and listening to the drum-like, spattering-staccato sounds of rain on the convertible top.

I scooted to the passenger seat and wiped steam from the window to look out at the gray facade of the enormous mansion. The six towering columns at the entrance dwarfed the oaks of the surrounding woods, and time had been kind: the shutters were drawn on the front windows against the coming winter, and their paint was chipped and peeling; the steps which led to the first landing were cracked and crumbling. But this was insufficient evidence that two decades had passed.

I was frightened now, looking out at the great, cold facade from the warm and secure familiarity of my car. In retrospect, it seems childishly unreasonable that in driving down from New York City I had hoped Harmer House would be smaller, hoped that, over the years, my imagination had added to its dimensions—as though my problem were directly proportional to the size of the place. But proportional or not, the mansion was a problem I had to face.

I thought about the letter I had received from the attorney, Mark Shorewood, informing me that I had inherited Harmer House. It wasn't altogether surprising that Mr. Harmer had remembered me in his will, but getting the house was unexpected and disconcerting—particularly since Mr. Harmer's sister, Edith, was still living there. It seemed strange that Mr. Harmer would will the family mansion to a near stranger, especially one he hadn't seen in almost twenty years. No doubt the attorney could clarify Mr. Harmer's actions, but I dreaded going inside to meet him, dreaded having to relive a part of my life that had been so painful.

The rain came down harder. Streams of water swirled over the cobblestones and down the U-shaped drive to the backwoods dirt road. It had been the cobblestones and columns that had impressed me most. How deeply they had impressed me! Cobblestones and columns; after nearly twenty years, a sensory return.

I remembered the smoothness of the cobblestones on my bare feet and my reeling with the heady sensation of standing beneath the columns and looking up in awe as they rose—seemingly a mile up—piercing the overhanging roof with their points.

I was only six years old then, and was living with my father, a sharecropper, on a rented farm three miles from Harmer House and fifteen miles from the small town of Blackston, Virginia. My mother had died the year before, and my father and I were living alone. Father was repairing the roof of the silo one day when he fell the two or three stories to the ground and lay twisted, unconscious. I was terrified. I stood frozen, looking down at him, not knowing what to do. Then instinctively I ran crying to Harmer House, ran the entire three miles.

The Harmers were our nearest neighbors—if one could call them that, for we had never visited them or even talked to them, but had only passed the mansion two or three times a week in my father's old flat-bed truck, singing as we always did. And occasionally father would point to the mansion and tell me that one day he would build me one just like it, and he would build me a throne covered with red velvet, and kings and queens would visit me.

So I ran crying to Harmer House. I climbed the steps and twisted the bell in the great door, crying for my father, crying for my feeling of helplessness, and crying for fear of what the huge mansion might hold. I almost ran when the little window in the door opened and two eyes peered out over my head, glanced from side to side, then finally down to me. The eyes stared curiously for a moment, then the window closed and the door swung open, framing a man dressed in black and white. He was the first butler I had ever seen, and as he bent down to me, saying something in a subdued and monotoned voice, I was transfixed by his silhouette against an enormous crystal chandelier which refracted more color and light than I had ever seen.

Sobbing, I told the butler what had happened to my father, the tears in my eyes multiplying the images of color and light from the chandelier. The butler took my hand and led me into the entrance hall. I scarcely looked at anything but the chandelier, but out of the corners of my eyes I could see the two staircases that joined to form a horseshoe shape, flanking the two-story, high-domed entrance hall. The butler took me through the darkened doorway of the library, and my feet could feel first the cool marble floor of the entrance hall, then the varnished wood flooring of the library, and finally the warmth of the rug upon which Mr. Harmer's desk rested.

I remember Mr. Harmer looking up, smiling and saying, "Well, what have we here?" I can still visualize his smile fading to an expression of concern as the butler related my story. Mr. Harmer rose from his desk, towered over me, then finally picked me up, telling the butler to send someone to the farm immediately and to get a doctor. Then I remember very little until—hours or days later —Mr. Harmer told me that my father had gone away and wouldn't be back any more. He asked me if I would like to live with him, and I told him that I would.

After that, days passed, days of vague images: Edith in her wheel chair, unfriendly, unsmiling, distant; long walks in the woods and countryside with Mr. Harmer who always wore his battered and faded straw hat which he called his walking hat; the black-and-white car that brought the sheriff on his periodic visits; and the last day at Harmer House, the day I was told that the authorities wouldn't let me stay there any longer because they said I needed both a mother and father, and Edith, confined to her wheel chair, couldn't care for me as properly as they thought I should be cared for.

There were tears in Mr. Harmer's eyes the morning the black-and-white car took me off to Kent County Orphanage. I remember his figure, waving, growing smaller as we drove away from the house. And what an ominous spectacle the orphanage seemed that early morning in contrast to Harmer House: low-silhouetted buildings, squat and gray, huddled together on barren ground. And children of all ages, dressed alike in faded blue uniforms, scurrying back and forth among the flat, ugly buildings in the morning chill. I had no way of knowing at the time that I would be rescued from the place within the year by my foster parents, the Gilmores, ultimately to live in New York City. I knew only that, with my father's death, my world had ended.

Harmer House seemed my only salvation, and the sheriff's car seemed my only link with Harmer House. The car was warm, and I didn't want to leave it. But, of course, I had no choice.

Now, nearly twenty years later, I was once again reluctant to leave a warm car. And I cursed myself for not taking the time to visit Mr. Harmer in all those years and for thinking that writing to him was enough and for promising him that one day I would visit him—and for not doing so. Now it was too late. Now he was dead, gone forever, and the meaning of the Russian Poet Yevtushenko's lament—that we pay tribute to the dead, and not the living—struck me with full and awful impact! Even in death Mr. Harmer had thought of me, and this weighed heavily on me as I sat looking at the mansion he had left in my name.

It was apparent that there would be no lull in the storm, so I draped my raincoat over my head and walked quickly up the cobblestone walk to the entrance. On the porch, I shook the rain from my coat and looked out from the columns. The countryside glistened with rain. I had forgotten how beautiful the country could be. The air was clear, and I could smell the damp earth and the fragrance of sassafras from the woods nearby. I took a deep breath and turned towards the door.

I no longer had to look up at the bell, and the small window in the door was almost at eye level. I twisted the bell handle and waited nervously. There was no answer, so I gave the bell another twist. Presently, the small window opened, and the bearded face and faded blue eyes of an old man appeared behind the wrought-iron framework of the window. I couldn't visualize the face of the man who had answered the bell those many years ago, and I didn't recognize this face, but it could have been the same man. The old man gazed at me, blinking, and said nothing.

"I'm Elizabeth Gilmore," I said.

The bearded face was impassive.

"Elizabeth *Jarrow* Gilmore," I said, emphasizing my father's name in hope that he might recognize it. "I have an appointment with Mr. Shorewood, the attorney."

The old man studied me closely, as though I were a stranger who had no business there, and for a brief moment I thought I detected fear in his eyes. "Yes," he finally said, and closed the window. A second later the door opened and the old man motioned impatiently for me to enter. "Wait here," he said sharply, and I stood in the entrance hall and watched him as he went into the library, closing the door behind him.

Chapter Two

The entrance hall was gloomy, dimly lit from a yellow candleflame-shaped bulb in a wall fixture at the opening of the west corridor. Owing to the storm-darkened sky, very little light penetrated the second-story stained-glass windows of the hall, and I could hardly perceive the outlines of the staircase banisters which wound into the second-story darkness. Overhead, the chandelier was dark and seemed much smaller than I remembered it. Its dusty, crystal prisms reflected only faintly the reds and greens and blues of the multicolored windows.

But nothing had changed. Across from the door were two antique chairs of dark mahogany and time-worn blue velvet, neither suitable nor comfortable for sitting. And centered beneath the chandelier was a long, rectangular inlaid table, a few unopened letters scattered across its top. The great high-domed hall looked as though it had never entertained a sharp sound or laughter—or life, for that matter! There was nothing else in the hall except an antique hat tree to the right of the front door. I hung my raincoat on the hat tree, and several seconds passed before

I realized that the object of my attention was Mr. Harmer's battered and faded straw walking hat.

A flood of memories came to me when I recognized the hat; memories of fishing at the creek with Mr. Harmer and of his laughing when I caught my first fish and was afraid to take it off the hook, and of my asking him to set it free again because I couldn't bear being responsible for its death. I was reaching out to touch the hat, to touch my past, when I was startled by a voice directly behind me. I hadn't heard the old man come out of the library. "I'll ask you not to touch that!" he said. And when I jerked my hand back, startled, he added, "Mr. Shorewood will see you now. He's in the library."

I was at once hurt and offended that the old man had interrupted my tryst with the past, and I was bent on re-establishing the link. "Was it you who answered the door the day of my father's death?" I asked.

He stared at me for a long moment, saying nothing. Like Mr. Harmer, he was tall and thin, and slightly stoop-shouldered. He had a full head of steel-gray hair, and his beard, too, was full, as Mr. Harmer's had been. "Yes, it was I," he said curtly. And then, as though to hurriedly dismiss the subject, he added, "You're keeping Mr. Shorewood waiting."

It didn't take much prompting for me to leave the old man to his rudeness. I turned towards the library just as a handsome young man emerged, smiling and extending his hand in greeting.

"Miss Gilmore," he said. "I didn't mean to keep you waiting here in the hallway."

He, too, was tall, but broad shouldered, athletically built, with a confident but gentle manner. His even white teeth shone brightly in contrast to a tanned face which belied the season, and his dark curly hair was unparted. "I'm Mark Shorewood," he said, taking my hand.

"I expected an older man, Mr. Shorewood," I said, not

thinking of anything else to say that wouldn't have sounded equally inane.

He laughed, a warm and pleasant baritone laugh that made me feel comfortable. "I think there must be a master pattern in the Platonic heavens for the well-wrought attorney whose image I simply don't fit," he said. "You're not the first to be surprised that I'm not an irascible old man. One day I'll live up to the image, though, I suppose."

I have no doubt that I'd still be standing there, looking into his blue eyes, had he not placed his hand on the small of my back and guided me toward the library. I was fascinated by him. He was one of the most attractive men I had ever seen, and I hoped that I had regained my composure enough so that my expression didn't make my thoughts obvious to him.

"Come in, Miss Gilmore," he said. "I was just about to have tea."

In contrast to the entry hall, the library was warm and well lighted. The furnishings were much the same as I remembered them. The walls were lined floor to ceiling with bookcases. Mr. Harmer's desk still rested on the large oval loop rug before the west-wall window. Occasional chairs and two small tables with lamps on them were in their customary places. The only change was several chairs grouped in a semi-circle around the fireplace. A serving cart was standing outside the semi-circle. Above the fireplace was a nicely framed print of Van Gogh's *Café Terrace at Night;* it had always had a strong emotional effect on me which I never questioned. I had forgotten, until that moment, that it was in Harmer House that I first saw the reproduction. Unconsciously, I must have associated it with Mr. Harmer and pleasant days following my father's tragic death. Unlike the entry way, too, which was sterile and musty smelling, the library smelled faintly of pine from the wood burning in the fireplace. I could feel my eyes moisten as I stood in almost the same spot where I

14

had first seen Mr. Harmer, and looked now at the library window at the changing patterns of rain drops whipped by the wind against the pane.

Mark Shorewood closed the door and motioned towards the semi-circle of chairs. "Have a seat by the fire," he said. "Would you like some tea?" I nodded, and he poured tea for both of us, taking a seat opposite mine. "Miss Harmer will join us shortly," he said. "Did you enjoy your trip from New York?"

"Yes. I enjoy driving, and it's good to get into the country again for a change."

"You're an editor, I understand."

"Yes, a magazine editor."

"I've always thought of editors as tweedy pipe smokers with patches on their elbows, not attractive redheads with large brown eyes," he said, smiling.

I laughed. "That goes with my image of attorneys as being old and irascible."

"Two stereotypes dispelled at first glance," he said. "What's the name of your magazine?"

"*Dégagé.* You probably haven't heard of it," I said, noting his quizzical expression. "It's a women's magazine—your wife would probably recognize the title."

"I'm not married."

"Oh," I said, resisting the urge to add, *good!* I took a sip of tea instead, watching him over the rim of my teacup as he glanced at the unringed third finger of my left hand.

We sat in silence for a while, neither of us feeling the obligation to pick up the lagging conversation. It's most unusual for two strangers to feel comfortable with one another in silence, but I was totally at ease with Mark Shorewood—as though I had known him all my life—and he seemed equally at ease with me. It was most comfortable sitting with him by the fire and listening to the rain spattering against the library windowpane.

"How long will you be staying?" he asked.

"Just the weekend. That is, if I can sign the papers right away."

"Well, I won't have them ready for your signature until Monday. If I had known that you were coming down, I could have had them ready for you—if you had called me yesterday, rather than this morning."

"I hadn't really planned on coming down so soon," I said. "It was a last-minute decision. It's really a bad time for me to get away, but my curiosity got the best of me."

"It will be several months before the estate is settled, but Miss Harmer says that you can take possession of the house as soon as she moves to Richmond. You're welcome to stay in the meantime, of course."

"No, I must get back—deadlines, you know. I would appreciate it, though, if I could sign the papers in time to leave early Monday afternoon."

"No problem. I'll have them for you by ten o'clock Monday morning."

"Fine," I said, then added, "I'm puzzled by the will. Did you draw it up?"

"Yes."

"I was wondering why Mr. Harmer left the house to me, instead of to his sister. And you mentioned her moving to Richmond. Is she moving on my account?"

"No, not at all. She's moving because she wants to move. The Harmers have always owned a smaller house in Richmond, and as soon as the present tenants vacate, she'll move in. This place is much too isolated and huge and cold for a woman her age to stay here alone. As for Mr. Harmer's leaving the house to you, well, he wanted you to have it. He decided when your father died that this would be your home, and he's finally going to have his wish. No, the house wouldn't be suitable for his sister, and she's the last of the Harmers."

"I wish I had known sooner. Did he have a long illness?"

Mark stared into the fire, seemingly distracted. I thought at first that he hadn't heard me until, after a long pause, he said, "He wasn't ill at all; his death was accidental."

"Oh, no! How did it happen?"

"It's just as well I tell you before Miss Harmer joins us," he said. "He fell from the staircase to the marble floor in the hallway."

"Good heavens!" The vision of my father falling through space came back to me with sickening clarity. "But how?"

"I don't know," Mark said. "It seems impossible, but that's what happened. Miss Harmer found him there about six o'clock one morning. There's no phone in the house—she won't allow it—and Harold, the caretaker who let you in, was out of town on a business errand for Mr. Harmer, so the poor woman had to wait more than an hour for the cook to arrive before they could send for a doctor—not that a doctor could have done any good. He was killed instantly."

I tried to keep talking, tried to keep from remembering the horribly sickening sound of my father's body hitting the ground, the sound that haunted me even now whenever I heard something heavy drop to a hard surface. "That's terrible," I said. "But the banisters are so high. . . ."

"I know. It had to be a freak accident. I used to go hiking in the countryside with him occasionally. He was more agile and sure-footed than I. Stranger things have happened, of course, but it's hard to accept when it happens to someone you know."

"I know. My father—"

"Yes, I know," Mark interrupted, apologetically. "I'm sorry I had to tell you, but I thought that you might have asked about him in front of Miss Harmer, and I don't think she could take it."

I must have had a sorrowful expression, for Mark came

17

over to me, patted my hand sympathetically, and picked up my teacup. "How about some more tea?" he asked.

"Thank you."

He filled my cup and brought it back to me, taking a seat beside me and grinning. "What's a nice girl like you going to do with a big place like this?"

His question was a light-hearted one to change the subject from the grim direction it had taken, but it touched the center of my problem and lightened my spirits very little. "I don't have the faintest idea, Mr. Shorewood."

"Call me Mark," he insisted.

"All right. Seriously, Mark, I'm deeply worried. I know that Mr. Harmer wanted me to have this place, and I appreciate it, but I couldn't possibly afford to keep it in repair. And living so far away. . . ."

"No need to worry about that. The estate will take care of maintenance and taxes. Mr. Harmer provided for that. And in the event of Miss Harmer's death, the rest of the estate will also go to you. It's a considerable amount, but because most of it is tied up in business investments and the Harmer Foundation, it's hard to tell what the liquid assets would amount to."

I had no time to think about Mark's last revelation, for we were interrupted by the opening of the library door, and my attention was drawn to Edith Harmer, who was being wheeled into the room by Harold. Her dark mourning clothes reminded me once again of Mark's troubled attitude towards Mr. Harmer's death. I had a strong, intuitive impression that Mark didn't really believe that Angus Harmer had fallen by accident!

Chapter Three

I was surprised at Edith's manner. She smiled when Mark introduced me, and she was very pleasant and gracious. I had remembered her as stern and aloof, unsmiling. But that was a child's impression, and long ago.

She told Harold to bring in my luggage, and when I told her that I had intended staying at the hotel in town, she wouldn't hear of it. She seemed genuinely eager for me to stay, and while I found the prospect distasteful in light of my conversation with Mark and the extreme isolation of the place, I couldn't refuse her. She was very charming and, at the time, I felt guilty for having misjudged her.

She was in her sixties and bore a strong resemblance to her brother. She was a thin woman with a long, angular face, high cheek bones and sharp features. But she was strikingly attractive. Her hair was apparently long, although she wore it combed back tightly in a bun. She was very alert, made quick gestures with her hands as she talked, and her dark, wide-set eyes missed nothing.

We had a pleasant chat, mostly about my job and New York City and my foster parents' trip abroad, until Mark finally rose to leave. Edith made him promise to return the next day for lunch, and I saw him to the door. I had hardly closed the door behind him when I was already looking forward to his return. I was beginning to embarrass myself with my schoolgirl adoration of him. But I found him irresistible.

After Mark left, Edith had Harold take me on a tour of the house before showing me to my room. I found that in addition to Harold there was only one other servant, a cook-housekeeper, whom Harold passed by without introduction or notice. I later learned that she wasn't a live-in servant.

The house was even larger than I remembered. It comprised two wings, with a kitchen, pantry and living room occupying the center of the first floor; and a large upstairs library occupying the center of the second. In the west wing of the first floor were the library where I had met Mark, the dining room, and Harold's quarters. Across the corridor from Harold's room was the kitchen, at the end of which was a narrow service stairway that led to the second-floor bedrooms. In the east wing were a game room and Edith's room.

We climbed the carpeted stairs from the entry hall. At the top was a landing where the two staircases joined and from which three more steps rose to the second floor. Harold stopped at the banister on the landing and looked to the marble floor below. "See here," he said, motioning for me to come to the banister. I stepped closer, looking at the chandelier which hung just below the banister level, and then down to the marble floor, shuddering as I did so, for I had always had a fear of heights. I could see nothing that Harold might have called my attention to, and I was wondering why he had called me to the banister when he finally pointed down and said, in a quiet monotone, "That's where they found him. Fell head first, right from this very spot, they figure! They knew he fell head first because—"

"Please!" I interrupted. "I don't want to hear about it!"

Harold turned abruptly and climbed the three steps to the landing. "I was out of town when it happened," he said over his shoulder. I made no reply, hoping that he would change the subject. He reached the top step and pointed towards the west wing. "Four guest rooms over there. Never used, though," he added. He walked past the central door. "Library," he told me, and walked down the hall to the east wing. "Mr. Harmer's room up front there. Hasn't been touched since his death. And this is your room," he said, opening the only other door on the west wing.

The bedroom was huge, with a high ceiling, faded wallpaper and an enormous Persian rug in the center of the polished hardwood floor. On the south wall were a fireplace, a writing desk, two chests of drawers and an overstuffed living room set, along with a coffee table and two end tables with lamps. The bed was on the opposite wall, and it was flanked by doors leading to a walk-in closet on one side and a bathroom with a sunken tub on the other. There were night stands with lamps on either side of the bed.

Although Harold had built a fire in the fireplace when he brought my luggage up, the room was very cold. By the size of it, I judged that it would take at least a month to heat it.

"Dinner will be ready at six," Harold said. "There's a buzzer on the bedside table. Ring for me if you need anything."

I stood in the center of the room for a long while after Harold left. I was terribly depressed by the place and had a strange, uncomfortable feeling about it. If it hadn't been for Edith's eagerness for me to stay, I would have thrown my luggage back into the car and gone to the hotel.

I began unpacking my suitcases and hanging my clothes in the closet to keep busy. Perhaps, I thought, I was being too sensitive. After all, it had been only two months since Mr. Harmer's death, and both Harold and Edith were probably still feeling the effects of the shock. There was certainly nothing at Harmer House to take their minds from the death either. That would explain Harold's preoccupation with Mr. Harmer's death and his unusual behavior on the landing. And, really, Mark didn't say that he thought the death anything other than a freak accident. The more I thought about it, the more impatient I grew with myself for becoming so depressed and suspicious.

After hanging my clothes up and putting my luggage away in the closet, I sat down on a chair near the fireplace for a moment and realized what a full day it had been. I had made the trip from New York to Virginia nonstop and had been in tense conversation ever since I arrived. I was tired. And for good reason.

Since I had little more than an hour before dinner, I realized that there was no time for a nap, so I decided to take a long hot bath. It was then I discovered that I couldn't lock my bedroom door. The lock was missing. There were two deep depressions in the wood where a bolt lock had been, and it looked as though the lock had been only recently removed. I didn't think much about it at the time but simply made a mental note to have Harold replace it after dinner. Meanwhile, I undressed in the bathroom while I drew my bath water. I looked forward to a hot bath and a few minutes' relaxation by the fireplace before dinner.

Harold served a fine *Cabernet Sauvignon* with our meal, and that, along with my hot bath and brief rest, added to my feeling of well-being. Edith was more reserved at dinner than she had been earlier in the day. But then dinner is generally the time for light, urbane conversation, and since Edith was pretty much a recluse one could hardly expect light conversation with a stranger to be her forte.

But I found her a frightening after-dinner speaker! We retired to the living room for coffee and brandy and discussèd my foster parents, who were in England on publishing business at the time. I was telling Edith how much I had wanted to make the trip with them, but that I couldn't arrange the necessary leave of absence from my job at the magazine to do so. I had always wanted to go to England, I told her, and had been interested in English castles since my childhood. Edith laughed, which perplexed me. There is something very frightening about laughter out of context, and I had said nothing, to my knowledge, to cause such laughter.

"Well," Edith said, "we can't offer you castles, but we *can* offer you the ghosts!"

I smiled, thinking it her attempt at humor. But when she simply stared at me, a serious expression on her face, and said nothing more, I interposed, "You're joking."

"Not at all."

I had heard numerous stories about resident ghosts haunting the old houses in upstate New York, stories related by very reputable and intelligent people, so I didn't discount them entirely. But I had always considered resident ghosts quaint and charming and, in any case, someone else's problem, not mine.

"Have you ever seen them?" I asked.

"Oh, yes," Edith assured me. "I've seen them many times. There used to be just one—the lady in white, I call her. I suspect that she's an ancestor. She moves around the house late at night. Carries a knife, you know."

"A knife?"

"It seems to be a knife. It's hard to tell, though. One only sees her fleetingly. Lately, of course, there's been Mr. Harmer." She made the statement with a chilling, matter-of-fact tone and manner.

"You're not serious!"

"But of course I'm serious, my dear. Do you take me for a fool? Do you think I'd joke about my poor dead brother?"

"No. I didn't mean. . . ."

"I should hope not," Edith retorted. "In the past few weeks we've seen him moving around the grounds. That is, I've seen him only once, but Harold has seen him many times."

She looked up as Harold entered the room and offered us more brandy, which I refused. "We were talking about Angus' ghost," she said to Harold.

Harold seemed momentarily upset, but he recovered quickly and coolly poured more brandy for Edith. "I've seen Mr. Harmer on numerous occasions," he said. "Mostly in the garden. But once I saw him on the drive near the road, and once in the entrance hall." He shook his head. "Very strange," he mumbled. "Very strange."

I was bewildered and frightened by their dispassionate discussion. It was as though they were talking about a rare species of bird they had seen flitting about their garden! Such talk quite naturally reminded me of my need for a lock on my bedroom door, and I asked Harold if he would replace the lock before retiring for the night.

"There *is* a lock on your door," he said emphatically. "A bolt lock."

"It's been removed."

"Impossible," Harold insisted.

"I don't mean to contradict you, but the lock is missing."

"Hmm," Harold mumbled, leaving the living room. "I'll have a look."

All during Harold's revelations about Angus Harmer's ghost, Edith sat back sipping her brandy and smiling self-contentedly. We both fell silent when Harold left the room, but his words were still hanging in the air, and I was examining and re-examining them for some semblance of sense when Edith broke the silence.

"If you'll excuse me, it's my bedtime," she said, backing

her wheel chair away from the fireplace. "The house is yours. Feel free to move about as you please."

Moving about the house was farthest from my intentions at the moment. I wanted only to lock myself safely in my room and not budge out of it until daylight. I decided to have another cup of coffee in order to give Harold time to fix the lock on my door.

I said good night to Edith and watched her maneuver her wheel chair adroitly through the living room to the door. She stopped at the doorway and pivoted to face me. "By the way, you needn't worry about the lock for your door. The cook goes home every night at six, and Harold's the only one who can go upstairs. He won't go up there unless you ring for him."

She turned her wheel chair and was gone before I had a chance to reply. I felt a little foolish at first, but on second thought, I figured that one would be foolish *not* to consider such things after being told that the place was haunted!

I waited a long time, but when Harold didn't return I assumed that he had replaced the lock and retired for the night. I wasn't the least bit sleepy now, so I decided to go to the library to get a book to read in my room.

The library was a godsend to me in my distraught state. Browsing through books is my favorite pastime, and I had never seen such a library. There were hundreds of first editions. I don't know how long I spent looking through the books—perhaps an hour or more. I was still deeply engrossed with them when I got the eerie feeling that someone was watching me. I was standing near the fireplace and I turned towards the door, thinking that Harold had perhaps entered the room and was waiting for me to look up so as not to disturb me. But there was no one at the door. I started to turn my attention once again to the book I was holding when, for some reason, I looked to the library window. Outside the window, standing in partial shadow and barely visible in the periphery of light which penetrated the darkness from the library, stood the dead Angus Harmer staring back at me!

I dropped the book and stood petrified. Never, until that moment, had I ever been paralyzed with fear. But now I knew the full and terrible meaning of the description. My throat constricted and I couldn't utter a sound. I just stood there, unable to take my eyes from the window that framed the frightening specter. He was wearing his walking hat and a navy blue woollen coat.

I have no idea how long we regarded each other. I knew only that, before I realized it, I was suddenly standing in the entrance hall, near the table under the chandelier, panting for breath. I don't even remember running from the library. My mind must have blacked out entirely, as though, unable to stand the reality of my frightening dilemma, it had simply stopped functioning. I had moved purely by reflex and found myself there, staring at the very spot on the marble floor where he had fallen to his death! And when my mind finally recorded the fact that I was staring at the spot, my fear found voice, and I ran screaming down the west corridor towards Harold's quarters so blind with terror that I ran headlong into Harold, sending us both sprawling to the corridor floor.

Harold got to his feet and helped me up. The jolt of our collision wrenched my hysteria from me, as though by coming into contact with something solid and real, I was re-established in the world of the living.

I don't recall what I told Harold in the panic of the moment; I remember only that he led me up the stairs to my room. I don't recall his trying to console me. I doubt that he did. I was calmed only by his presence, by the fact that I wasn't alone. And even then, in retrospect, there wasn't much comfort in this strange man leading me through a strange house to my strange bedroom. I felt terribly alone and lost, and the only thing that helped me maintain my sanity in that dark moment was the knowledge that Mark was returning the next day—a fact that I dwelled upon, trying to keep my mind from straying back to the library and the ghost of Angus Harmer.

The effect of fear on the mind is incredible. Days after that incident, my mind played back bits of the dialogue with Harold like a tape recorder. It was as though my mind had recorded everything but hadn't registered it in my consciousness. I remember my constant pleading for Harold to take me to my car instead of my room. I don't recall asking him to do so at the time, but in a more rational moment that's exactly what I would have asked.

By the time he got me to my room, I was beginning to recover from the shock. As he closed my door on his way out, I noticed that he hadn't replaced the lock.

"The lock!" I shouted. "You promised to replace it!"

He reappeared in the doorway and looked at me with disdain. "Can't," he said. "I'll have to get another one in town tomorrow."

"Tomorrow! Surely there must be another lock in the house somewhere!"

"No," he said coolly, "there isn't. This is the only door in the house that takes a bolt lock. The rest of them have regular locks—this one does, too, but it doesn't work. That's why I put a bolt lock on there a couple of years ago. Besides, nobody's going to come into your room."

He slammed the door behind him without another word. No doubt he was indignant because my insistence upon a lock for my door implied that I thought he might enter unannounced, for he was the only one in the house at night who could do so. I didn't detain him any longer because I suddenly feared him. He was obviously lying about the lock; the impression the removed lock had made on the door and sash was down to the unfinished wood, and there were many layers of stain and varnish around it. Clearly, he hadn't recently added the lock. It had always been on the door!

27

I searched the room thoroughly, turning on every light. I even searched under the bed. There was no one in the room. How I wished for a telephone—I would have called Mark to come and get me out of the house. As it was, I was too afraid to even step across the hall to get a book from the upstairs library, let alone walk down the dimly lit corridor and down the stairs and across the marble floor upon which Mr. Harmer had fallen to his death and into the darkness to my car in an effort to escape the wretched place.

I paced the floor for a while before realizing that I had to get my mind off the house and everyone in it. I had nothing to read, so I got stationery from my luggage and sat down at the writing table by the fireplace. I wouldn't dream of mailing the letter to my parents which I would write in such a state of terror, but I had to be doing something.

I had been writing for a long while when I heard a faint tapping at the door. I called out, but there was no answer. Thinking that perhaps the tapping I heard was partially my imagination and partially the storm sounds which were building in intensity outside my bedroom window, I resumed writing. But the tapping came again—this time louder and with a rhythmic beat that precluded its being storm noises. Someone was definitely knocking on my door. Again I called out, and again there was no answer. I went to the door, thinking that it was Harold and that he probably couldn't hear my call over the storm sounds. Just as I reached the door, someone knocked again. I called through the door and, hearing no reply, I cautiously opened it.

There was no one there!

Chapter Four

The hallway was dark, save for the widely spaced and tiny yellow candle-flame bulbs that barely illuminated the wall fixtures which contained them. From my doorway I could see the length of the hallway in both directions. To my right, toward the service stairs, the hall was enveloped in almost total darkness. To my left, I could see the second-story banister that bordered the high-domed entry hall, the top of the chandelier which hung from the ceiling and the door to the front west-wing bedroom. There was no movement. I listened for footfalls on the stairs but could hear nothing.

I closed the door and rang for Harold. I thought he had no doubt knocked and failed to hear my call through the heavy bedroom door. I waited for perhaps five minutes and rang again, thinking that he might not have had time to return to his room. But I had no sooner rung the second time than I again heard a knock on my door. I opened it cautiously. Harold stood in the doorway, disgruntled and sleepy-eyed, his hair unkempt, his hands plunged deeply into the pockets of his robe. He appeared to have just awakened, and he stood looking at me through heavy-lidded, cold blue eyes. He was obviously perturbed.

"It's after midnight!" he said.

"Yes, I know, but I was awake when you knocked a few

minutes ago and you apparently didn't hear me call to you."

He looked at me in bewilderment for a moment. "I don't know what you're talking about," he said.

"I called to you when you knocked on my door a while ago, but—"

"Miss Gilmore," Harold interrupted, irritated, "I've been asleep for nearly two hours, and you just awakened me from that sleep!"

"But someone knocked on my door several times before I rang for you. I assumed. . . ."

"Other than you and me," he said, "there's only one other person in the house. And since she happens to be a paraplegic, it's highly unlikely that she climbed the stairs in her wheel chair and knocked on your door! And while I sympathize with your emotional problem, I'll thank you not to impose that problem upon *me*. Good night!"

I was confounded by his sarcasm and was at a loss to answer him as he turned and disappeared into the darkness towards the service stairs. His lack of sympathy wasn't inconsistent, but his insulting behavior and lack of respect was uncalled for.

I closed the door and again sat down at the writing table. Looking at my stationery, I realized that my mind had long since rebelled against the idea of recording my experience with the ghost of Angus Harmer. My distraught state had robbed me of the concentration and discipline I needed for organized thought. I was amazed to see that my letter had trailed off into a series of strange doodles consisting of webs with spiders in them, a curious abstract scrollwork of intricate and well-executed design far beyond my draftsmanship ability; and, finally, the name Julia Carter written repeatedly in a handwriting that was not my own!

I stared at the paper as though seeing it for the first time. It must have been the work of my subconscious mind, for I had never seen the design before, and the name Julia Carter meant nothing to me. I wondered if there was a connection between my seeing the ghost of Angus Harmer and the cryptic handiwork on my stationery. I wondered, too, if someone or some force had been guiding my hand! I shuddered and crumpled the paper up in an effort to remove its strange contents from my mind. This weird occurrence smacked of the supernatural to me. Indeed, there could hardly be a logical explanation for it. It had a chilling effect upon me, and I got up from the writing table and drew a chair before the fireplace for warmth.

The rain continued to beat heavily against my bedroom window, and my nerves were so frayed that the sharp crack of the lightning and endless rumble of the thunder made me jump at each report. I put another log on the fire and watched the flames arch around it until it was sufficiently warmed to catch fire. I became lost in thought as I tried to unravel my feelings and responses from the knotty complexities I had faced in the past few hours, and the frightening sounds of the raging storm finally receded from my consciousness. Perhaps Harold was right, I thought. Maybe seeing Angus Harmer's ghost and my fear of the strange house had caused me to imagine that I'd heard a tapping at my bedroom door. It might well have been the acoustics of the old house, the creaking of eaves or the flapping of loose shingles on the roof overhead that sounded like someone tapping. And even if Harold had lied about the lock, he had certainly not lied about being asleep. No one could possibly fake the puffy-eyed look and pallor that results from the decreased metabolic rate of sleep. No doubt he had sufficient reason to be irritated at my waking him. But that was no reason for his questioning my mental health. Had I said or done something after seeing the ghost in the library window to make him feel that I had taken leave of my senses? Probably so. Still, how else would he expect a person to act having just seen a dead man staring through a window?

The more I thought about it, the more intolerant I became of Harold's unreasonable judgment of me. And I was brooding about this when I again heard the tapping. It wrenched me from my introspection, and I listened carefully in order to determine its origin. It was the same, evenly spaced, rhythmic beat, eight or ten sharp raps, then a pause as though someone were waiting for an answer, followed again by eight or ten sharp raps.

I got up from my chair and tiptoed to the door. I placed my ear to the door and waited. Not a sound. I wondered if one could hear the tapping only at the fireplace—perhaps the sound was being carried by the masonry of the fireplace from the roof. I was about to take my ear from the door when the sound came again, extremely loud in my ear, the sound of knuckles against the wood. There *was* someone at my door!

"Harold?" I called. There was no answer, but I heard what sounded like the creaking of loose floor boards in the hallway near my door. I called louder: "Is that you, Harold?" Still, there was no answer.

I opened the door a crack and peeked out. I could see no one, but there was a strange fragrance in the air, a sweet, camphorous odor. I opened the door wider and peered down the hallway towards the service stairs in the back—the route Harold would have taken. Again, no one. I turned to look towards the front of the house, but before I could focus my eyes in that direction, I detected movement. Someone had rounded the corner of the library just as I turned my head and was apparently walking along the open corridor towards the west-wing bedrooms.

It didn't occur to me that my illusive visitor might not have been Harold. I walked quickly down the hallway in pursuit, and into the open corridor, taking several steps toward the west wing before I was frozen in horror by the

32

specter before me. The door to one of the bedrooms was open, and a woman with long blonde hair and dressed in a floor-length white wedding gown with a heavy veil over her face was standing in the doorway against the darkness of the unlighted bedroom.

I gasped when I saw her. She had her back to me, and she turned slowly to face me. There was a small rip in the front of her gown, and the area around the rip was stained, a rust color—like dried blood! I couldn't see through her veil, but I knew that she was looking at me. She stood motionless, her left hand resting on the doorknob, until she raised her right hand, and the flash of shiny metal shone from the blade of the knife she was holding!

A low, thick-bubbly, throaty laugh erupted from behind the veil, and she began moving slowly towards me, raising the knife higher as she approached. My heart pounded, and the camphorous odor grew thicker in the air.

"What are you doing?" I asked. "Who *are* you?"

Again there was the low, gurgling laughter, a haunting, terrifying, almost animal sound. For a mad moment, I considered striking out at her. Then, without taking my eyes from her, I lunged for the stairway and descended the three steps to the landing where the staircases joined. Feeling behind me for the banister and finding it, I backed down two or three steps of the east stairway, wishing that I had taken the west stairway which would have been closer to Harold's room. But she didn't follow me. She stopped at the head of the stairs, dropped the hand in which she held the knife and shook me again with her low, hideous laugh.

Outside, the lightning split the sky with a deafening crack, illuminating the stained glass windows above the entrance hall and laminating the woman's white gown in eerie green and blue and blood-red. Then as the thunder rumbled across the heavens with the dying of the lightning, the house was again plunged into semi-darkness, and I strained my eyes to accustom them to the relative gloom in order to keep sight of the knife-wielding menace on the stairs above me. But with the sound of the thunder she turned and glided slowly across the open corridor to the west-wing bedroom and swept inside as the heavy door closed soundlessly behind her.

I stood petrified, staring at the dark mahogany door and clutching the banister. I tried desperately to fight the weakness and dizziness that threatened to overcome me. My mind was stunned by the assault. I leaned against the banister for support and backed down the stairs keeping my eye on the door until I reached the bottom of the stairway, where I turned and ran screaming across the marble floor and down the hall to Harold's room. I hammered against Harold's door with both fists, crying for him to open it, pleading with him to hurry for fear that the woman might follow me.

Finally I heard the lock on the door click, and Harold jerked the door open, his eyes ablaze with anger. But he had no time to protest my intrusion, for with incredible strength I pushed him aside and plunged into his room. I was sobbing and trying to talk, and my body was trembling beyond control until he slapped me sharply across the face. My head cleared suddenly, and anger replaced my fear momentarily until I realized that he had slapped me from my hysteria. I sank to a rocking chair before his fireplace.

"What's the meaning of this, Miss Gilmore?" Harold asked.

"A woman," I blurted, still sobbing. "Upstairs. She has a knife!"

"What?"

"She went into one of the bedrooms in the west wing."

Harold sat down heavily in a chair opposite mine and looked at the clock on the mantle as though hoping it would say ten o'clock and that he'd have a full night's sleep ahead of him. But it was three-thirty. He rubbed his reddened eyes and sighed.

"Miss Gilmore, I told you that there are only three of us in the house and that. . . ."

"I don't care what you *told* me!" I shouted. "I saw a woman—the lady in white—and she came after me with a knife at the top of the stairs!"

"The lady in white," Harold repeated without emotion or conviction. He nodded, rose from his chair, shuffled tiredly to his desk and rummaged through the contents of the top drawer, mumbling to himself about the lady in white. He finally found a leather key ring, and walked towards the door, motioning for me to follow him.

"Come along," he said. "Let's have a look at your lady in white."

"She's armed!"

"Yes, so you told me," Harold said, as though talking to an imaginative child.

"You don't believe me!" I said, following him down the hall to the west stairway. Harold said nothing, but climbed the stairs, finally stopping before the doors of the west-wing bedrooms.

"Which door?" he said, impatiently.

"That one," I said, pointing to the door through which the woman had gone.

"Would you like to try opening it?" he said.

I backed away. "I'm telling you, she has a knife!"

"You'd find it locked, Miss Gilmore," he said, grabbing the doorknob and turning it vigorously to show me that it was locked. "The housekeeper opens them every couple of weeks or so to dust them and air them out," he added, fumbling with his key ring and squinting at the numbers on the keys. Finding the key, he unlocked the door and swung it open.

It was pitch dark inside, but Harold entered without the slightest hesitation and turned on a lamp. The room appeared to be empty, and I ventured in, cautiously. There was a strong fragrance of camphor in the air.

"Do you smell that?" I asked.

"What?"

"That odor. Camphor, I think it is."

Harold sniffed. "Yes," he said. "It's probably the disinfectant the housekeeper uses."

"But I smelled it in the hallway, too, when I first saw her, and I didn't smell it out there just now."

"Well it couldn't be anything else," Harold said. "Are you quite satisfied that there's no one in the room now?"

"Aren't you going to search the room?"

Harold sighed heavily. "If you insist, Miss Gilmore."

He searched the room thoroughly but found nothing to indicate that anyone had recently occupied it. He paid no attention when I suggested that the lady in white could have left the room when I went down to get him. He switched the lights off and closed the door behind us, checking to be sure that it was locked. "I'll see you to your room," he said.

We went to my room. I asked Harold to go in with me and to check it as well. Every light in the room was still burning and nothing had been disturbed. I was putting my raincoat on when Harold emerged from checking the bathroom.

"What are you doing?" he asked.

"I'm leaving. I'm not staying in this house another minute. I want you to see me out to my car; I'm taking a room at the hotel."

"I'm afraid I can't permit that," he said.

"What do you mean, you can't *permit* it?"

"There's a storm raging outside, Miss Gilmore, and these back roads are very dangerous—particularly at night. I can't be responsible for letting you leave in your present condition."

"I'll assume that responsibility." And as for my *present condition,* as you put it, that's exactly why I'm leaving!"

"I'm sorry," Harold said firmly, "but I can't let you go."

"Are you trying to tell me that I'm a prisoner here?"

"A prisoner?" Harold repeated, arching one eyebrow and looking at me curiously. "Not at all. A guest, Miss Gilmore, a very upset and emotional guest who shouldn't be turned out in a raging storm. As our guest, we do have a responsibility for your welfare."

"If you were the least concerned for my welfare, you'd help me get out of here!"

"Quite the contrary. You'll be quite safe at Harmer House."

I was speechless for a moment, and beginning to wonder about *Harold's* sanity.

"Safe?" I exclaimed. *"Safe?* I've seen a dead man; I've been chased through the halls by a ghost wielding a knife; I can't even lock my bedroom door, and you think I'll be *safe* at Harmer House! Have you seen this ghost . . . this lady in white?"

Harold stared at me for a moment, then turned and walked to the door. "I'll leave you now," he said. "I must get some sleep. I'd advise you to do the same."

"Why won't you talk about her?" I asked, following him to the door. "Why do you avoid answering my questions and ignore my comments about her?"

Harold turned at the doorway. He looked extremely tired. "About whom?" he said.

"Will you stop playing games with me? You know very well about whom! I'm talking about the lady in white. Can't you see that I'm being driven out of my mind by these ghosts!?"

"We can discuss that tomorrow," Harold said. "It's late."

I couldn't believe that anyone could be so lacking in compassion. I studied his face, but he averted my stare, as though he felt guilt for his dispassionate treatment of me. The pale yellow light of the hallway accented his deep wrinkles and fatigue from loss of sleep. He gave no sign of concern for my plight.

"I have no intention of being here to discuss it tomorrow," I said. "I'm leaving tonight. Now."

"That's your prerogative," he said, staring at the floor. "But you'll have to do so without my assistance. It'll be daylight in a couple of hours. I'd advise you to wait until then before leaving."

He turned without looking up at me, and I stood in the doorway and watched him walk tiredly towards the back stairs. I had intended to leave my belongings in the house and get Mark to bring me back to get them, but Harold's point about it being very close to daylight was a valid one.

I looked down the hall and shuddered at the thought of again seeing the lady in white, or of running across the ghost of Angus Harmer in the dark grounds outside. It would be far better to wait until daylight and to take my things with me, leaving the wretched place for good. I closed the door and began packing my clothes. By waiting for daylight, I could check into the hotel, look up Mark's number, and call him.

It was a little after four when I finished packing. It had been good to have my hands busy and my mind occupied. I put another log on the fire and paced the floor for a while, but fatigue finally overcame me, so I got a blanket from the bed, wrapped it around me, and curled up in the chair before the fireplace, facing the door. I could hardly wait for dawn to break. The minutes dragged unmercifully. I'd contact Mark, I thought, then I'd leave for New York as soon as I was rested.

Regardless of Angus Harmer's last wishes, I had no intention of taking possession of Harmer House. I wanted only to get away from it before it took possession of me!

Chapter Five

My head dropped, then snapped upright by reflex, awakening me with a start. I was terribly groggy and stiff, and it took me several seconds to get my bearings. I thought I had dozed momentarily, and I was again stricken with terror when I realized that someone could have entered the room as I slept. There was no one in the room with me, but in looking about the room, I noticed first that the fire was almost out, but also that the room seemed brighter. I glanced over my shoulder at the window and was overjoyed to see daylight.

Throwing the blanket from me, I got unsteadily to my feet and went to the window. My legs ached from the cramped position I had slept in and my head ached from strain and emotional tension. I was relieved to see that it had stopped raining, but the sky was gray and there were more black storm clouds gathering on the horizon. I looked at my watch. It was nearly eight o'clock. I hadn't merely dozed off; I'd slept for nearly four hours!

My sleep had been therapeutic in dispelling the dark thoughts that had troubled my mind, as daylight had dispelled the darkness that enveloped Harmer House like a shroud. Still, in my morning mind, dark thoughts and memories edged from somewhere in my subconscious to gather on the horizon of my consciousness menacingly—incidents of hours past, incidents as ethereal and as impossible to grasp as the mist that forms the clouds.

I scanned the grounds below my window as the thoughts gathered. It seemed incredible to me that the Eden-like beauty of the Harmer estate could be the augur of such evil. Even in the dinginess of inclement weather, the grounds were beautiful. The well-kept lawn was bordered by a low stone wall, and beyond the wall an expanse of meadow rolled gently towards the woods. The place would have been a beautiful retreat for weekends and summer vacations, but Harmer House had died with Angus Harmer just as my castle with the red-velvet throne had died with my father. It was bitter irony that they had both fallen to their deaths, and bitter irony that after nearly twenty years of trying to recover from the trauma of the first tragedy, I should have to be a party to the second.

Turning from the window, I focused my attention to my clothes. I was an absolute mess. I had slept in my raincoat, and I could hardly find a square inch of material in my dress that wasn't wrinkled. I thought about changing and freshening up before leaving, then noted with mild amusement that vanity had done for me what my courage had failed to do—it had momentarily overcome my fear of Harmer House and my longing to escape the place immediately!

I got my bags, closed the door behind me and walked quickly and quietly along the hallway to the stairs. The gray daylight had brightened the stained-glass windows enough to bathe the staircases and entry hall with their colors, and I smelled the aroma of freshly brewed coffee. There was life and activity in the house, and I felt more confident as I glanced quickly to the dreaded west-wing mahogany door at the end of the open corridor and descended the stairway.

No one saw me leave the house. I was relieved and thankful for that, for I didn't want to explain my departure to Edith, nor did I feel in the mood to talk to anyone. Once outside, I felt free again. I breathed the clean morning air and gave a sigh of relief as I put my luggage in the trunk and got into the car. When I locked the doors from the inside, I felt safe at last. I fumbled through my purse looking for my car keys and, finding them, I made a stab at inserting the key in the ignition. The night had taken its toll on my nervous system, for my hands were still trembling. I turned the ignition on, pulled the choke out, and pressed the starter button. The starter chattered rapidly, but the engine failed to start. I pushed the choke in and again tried to start the car, but the engine refused to turn over.

Turning the ignition off, I sat back in a conscious effort to regain my composure. In my panic to get on my way, I thought I had done something wrong—perhaps flooded the engine. After a few minutes, I tried to start the car again, going through each step in the starting procedure methodically, as I had once done when learning to drive. But still the engine wouldn't take hold; and I panicked, pressing the starter button until the starter began growling slower and slower, finally failing to respond at all.

I leaned back in anguish and closed my eyes. It seemed that the heavens themselves were conspiring to keep me at Harmer House! Tears of frustration welled in my eyes. Once more I found myself crying and alone before the great facade of the wretched place! It was like a terrifying and recurring nightmare. I was twenty years older now, but no less helpless or afraid.

The tears were streaming down my cheeks. I was blotting at them, my eyes closed, still slumped in the driver's seat, when someone rapped sharply on the window. Startled, I looked up to see Harold leaning down to peer at me, a great, black umbrella hovering over his head despite the fact that it wasn't raining. I rolled the window down.

"I've been looking all over for you," he said. "You

weren't in your room, and I noticed that your bags were gone."

"I can't get my car started. I must have run the battery down. Could you give me a push?"

Harold shook his head. "Can't," he said. "The station wagon's in town being serviced."

"Maybe the cook could help me, then."

"She doesn't have a car. Her husband drops her off and picks her up in the evening. I won't have the station wagon until tonight when I ride into town with the cook and her husband. Why don't you come to breakfast and give the battery time to build up again? Miss Harmer is waiting for you."

"I wanted to go into town now," I insisted.

"There's no way, except maybe when Mr. Shorewood comes to lunch. He might have a jumper cable or tow line."

Under the circumstances, there was little else I could do, so I followed Harold in. Edith was at the far end of the dining-room table sipping orange juice as I entered. I hung my coat and purse on the back of my chair and sat down. Edith looked up with a pleasant smile, taking no apparent notice of my obvious disheveled appearance or tear-reddened eyes.

"Well," she said brightly, "I see Harold finally found you. You're up early. Taking a walk?"

"Didn't Harold tell you I was leaving?" I said, pouring myself a cup of coffee. "I'd be gone, but my car wouldn't start."

"Leaving?" Edith said, surprised. "You don't mean you're leaving Harmer House?"

"Yes. I'm taking a room at the hotel in town."

"I won't hear of it," Edith said. "Why on earth should you pay for a room when we have a whole house full of rooms? Is there something wrong?"

"Under the circumstances, I should hardly think you'd expect me to stay any longer."

"What circumstances?" Edith said with an expression of concern. "I don't understand."

"Didn't Harold tell you anything—about last night, I mean? I was sure that the racket must have disturbed you."

"No. I haven't talked to Harold this morning, except when he told me that you weren't in your room and that he didn't know where you were."

"I saw the ghosts last night," I said. "Both of them."

Edith laughed. I was astonished at her laughter.

"Nightmares," Edith chuckled. "Surely you wouldn't leave us because you had nightmares? You were overtired. And then, of course, a strange bed in a strange house. . . ."

"They weren't nightmares, Miss Harmer. They were exactly as you described them, your brother and the lady in white. I was never so frightened in my life! The lady in white threatened me with a knife!"

Edith stared at me in disbelief. "As I *described* them?" she said.

"Yes. You and Harold."

"*Ghosts?*" Edith said. "For heaven's sake! I said nothing about ghosts—nor did Harold, to my knowledge. It must have been part of your dream, my dear. You must have been terribly exhausted from your trip."

It must have taken a full minute for her words to register, and even then I couldn't believe what I had heard. I looked at her searchingly, studying her to see if there was evidence that this was her idea of a bizarre, practical joke. But she was serious. I thought perhaps she was getting senile.

"It was after dinner," I said. "We were talking about English castles. You told me about the ghost—the lady in white, you called her—about how she carried a knife. Surely you remember?"

At first Edith stared at me quizzically as I began recounting our previous night's conversation, but soon her expression changed to one of sadness, and she finally shook her head, as though in pity, when I had finished talking.

"Just like Julia," she said. "You poor thing. You're just like her. She wanted to leave, too."

"Julia?" I blurted, suddenly remembering the name I had written in a strange hand on my stationery. "Do you mean Julia *Carter?*"

The pity vanished instantly and Edith's eyes flashed. "How do you know that?" she snapped. "How do you know that name? You couldn't possibly know that name!"

"I don't know," I said, and I was about to relate the strange circumstances by which I had learned the name, but Edith's expression stopped me. It was an extraordinary expression, one of enlightenment and fear—as though I had made a sudden and frightening revelation. We both fell silent for a moment until Edith regained her composure. Since I had said nothing to her except that I didn't know how I had come to know the name Julia Carter, I was most bewildered by her reaction.

"There are no ghosts at Harmer House, Miss Gilmore," she finally said.

"But it was *you* who told me about them!"

"No. You're mistaken," she said flatly, fixing me with her quick, dark eyes and an expression which told me that it was useless for me to pursue the matter further. Her eyes were still fixed upon me when Harold entered with covered platters of bacon and eggs, setting a dish before each of us and removing the covers. The sight of the food made me slightly nauseous.

Edith's manner changed completely.

"Did you know that Miss Gilmore tried to leave us this morning?" she said to Harold brightly.

"Yes, her car wouldn't start."

Edith began eating. "She had nightmares," she said. "About ghosts."

"I'm sorry to hear that," Harold said, refilling our coffee cups. "No doubt she was troubled by the storm. The thunder was terrible last night. Woke me up several times, too."

I was angered, and wondered if they were playing a macabre game at my expense. "It wasn't the thunder, as you well know!" I said to Harold.

He looked at me blankly. "I beg your pardon?" he said.

"We were to discuss the lady in white this morning, if you recall."

"The lady in white?" Harold repeated, shaking his head. "No, I don't recall, Miss Gilmore. I haven't the faintest idea what you're talking about."

"The lady in white!" I insisted. "Are you trying to make me believe that I woke you twice and had you searching the west-wing bedroom because of a nightmare? Do you think you're dealing with a child!"

Harold seemed genuinely shocked and puzzled. "I don't wish to offend you, Miss Gilmore, but I truly don't know what to say. Are you serious?"

"She's quite serious," Edith interrupted. "And she seems to think that we had a conversation about ghosts last night. Do you recall our discussing ghosts last night, Harold?"

"With *me*, Miss Harmer?"

"Yes, Harold, with *you!*" I said. "We were in the living room after dinner, and you said that you had seen the ghost of Mr. Harmer several times on the grounds and in the entry hall. And Miss Harmer spoke of the lady in white, said she was an ancestor or something!"

Harold looked at me, then at Edith, then back at me again, as though I had been speaking a foreign language that he didn't understand. He seemed at a complete loss for words and didn't bother to reply. Edith, too, simply stared at me, her expression grim, her eyes unblinking. She was quite obviously upset.

She backed her wheel chair from the table and moved towards the door, stopping at my end of the table in passing.

"You're our guest," she said in a voice shaking with emotion. "But I'll thank you not to mention my brother's name again in my presence so long as I'm mistress of Harmer House. The tragedy of his death was unbearable. Your references to his ghost are even *more* unbearable!"

I had been stunned so many times, Edith's words had little effect upon me. I didn't even bother to look up as she left the room. I simply sat, staring at the position at the table she had occupied, and listening to the receding slapping sounds of her hands against the wheels of her wheel chair until the room was silent. How she could lie to me and be so self-righteous about it was totally beyond my comprehension. But the question was *why* she was doing it—or why *they* were doing it, really. Harold was most certainly a party to the conspiracy. I was no longer furious with them, but curiously detached. I suppose my sudden detachment was nature's way of compensating for the unreality.

I turned to Harold, whose eyes were still fixed on the door after Edith's departure. "I was probably in error for speaking of Mr. Harmer's ghost in Edith's presence," I said. "But I assumed that since she spoke so candidly of him last night she had adjusted to the fact of his death. Did you avoid the truth for her sake just now?"

"I've known and worked for the Harmers for thirty years, Miss Gilmore, and I've never found it necessary to avoid the truth in their presence for any reason."

"Then why did you lie to me just now?"

"I didn't, madam."

"Do you recall my conversation with Miss Harmer last

46

night about my parents' trip abroad and about my fascination with English castles?"

"No," Harold said.

"Perhaps you weren't in the room at the time. Do you recall my asking you to replace the lock on my door?"

"No. I don't recall that either. But I wouldn't have understood if you had. There is a lock on your door, a bolt lock."

"That's exactly what you told me last night, and also that you couldn't replace it because mine was the only door in the house with a bolt lock."

"Every bedroom in the house has a bolt lock—including yours."

"Mine is missing."

"That's absolutely impossible!"

"How do you know? Have you checked it?"

"I have no reason to check it. I'm the only one in the house who could remove it, and I didn't."

"Would you mind coming up and checking it now?"

"If you insist," Harold said impatiently.

I got my raincoat and purse, and Harold followed me up the stairs. It was important for me to confront him with the only tangible evidence I had that our conversation of the night before had taken place. But as we climbed the stairs to my room, I was suddenly overwhelmed with self-doubt. There was no reasonable motivation for Edith denying our conversation or for Harold's denial. And I wondered if I had indeed slept all night in the chair before the fireplace and dreamed everything. Had my return to Virginia and to Harmer House brought back nightmarish fears of my youth so real that I thought I actually lived them?

No, I thought, it was impossible. I had seen the ghosts of Harmer House; and Harold and Edith, for some inexplicable reason, were now trying to cover up the fact that the ghosts of Harmer House existed. And in doing so, they were denying my own waking existence in the past twelve hours! Worse yet, I was being forced into the ridiculous position of having to verify my existence by pointing out something that didn't exist—a bolt lock. If the situation hadn't been so grim, it would have been laughable.

Harold followed me into my room, and I swung my door closed to show him that the lock was missing and that, in the face of such evidence, that part of my story, at least, couldn't be denied. But to my dismay, there was indeed a bolt lock on my door! Harold stood by patiently without a word, not the least surprised to see the lock, as I looking at it, stood completely stupified.

"Someone's replaced it since I left the room this morning," I said, groping for an explanation.

"No," Harold said.

"But I tell you, it was *missing!*"

"If you'll look closely," he said, "you'll see that the bolt is held in place by wood screws and that the screws are covered with layers of varnish from countless refinishings. In order to get the lock off, one would have to dig the old stain and varnish from them. Obviously the lock has never been taken from the door."

He was quite right. In fact, the screws were barely visible. I was astonished.

"You can think what you like about the lock," I said. "And since you weren't with me when I saw Mr. Harmer and the lady in white, you may think what you like about that too. But certainly you can't deny my knocking you down in the hallway last night or my asking you to open the west-wing bedroom this morning!"

Harold thought for a moment, and then, avoiding my gaze as though he didn't wish to embarrass me, he said. "Sometimes, Miss Gilmore, I've had dreams so vivid that I actually thought they were real—that is, until I awakened. I guess we all have them. I've heard that there's a thin line between fantasy and reality, but it never occurred to me

Latest U.S. Government
tests of all cigarettes
show True is
lower in both
tar and nicotine
than 98% of all other
cigarettes sold.

Think about it.
Shouldn't your next cigarette be True?

Regular: 12 mg. "tar", 0.8 mg. nicotine,
Menthol: 12 mg. "tar", 0.7 mg. nicotine, av. per cigarette, FTC Report Aug. '72.

Latest U.S. Government
tests of all menthol
cigarettes show
True is lower
in both tar and
nicotine than 98% of
all other menthols sold.

Think about it.
Shouldn't your next cigarette be True?

that a person could mistake his dream world for his real world. I guess it happens, though, and I figure that's what happened to you.

"After dinner last night," he continued, "I went into town to play cards with my brother-in-law and a few friends—as I usually do every Friday night. I left the station wagon in town for servicing, and rode back to Harmer House this morning with the cook and her husband."

"You rode back this morning?"

"Yes. I stayed the night at my brother-in-law's. So you see, Miss Gilmore, you couldn't possibly have awakened me last night. I wasn't even in the house."

Chapter Six

Harold's words totally destroyed the reality of the world I had inhabited for the previous twelve hours. And I found my dilemma so appallingly abstract that it was impossible for me to grapple with it.

I sent Harold down to get my baggage from the car so that I could bathe and change in order to be presentable when Mark came to lunch. In the time that Harold was gone, I pondered my problem, searching for an explanation more satisfactory to me than his. But I gave up in anguish. When he returned, I apologized to him and asked him to convey my apologies to Edith as well. I did so from amenity, rather than conviction. I needed time to think. I was so confused that, had I awakened to the alarm clock in my apartment in New York at that very moment to find that it had all been a dream—that I had not inherited Harmer House, had not driven to Virginia, had not met Mark Shorewood, had not, in fact, done any of the things I thought I had done in the past twenty-four hours—I would have been no less astonished and disconcerted.

When Harold left, I locked my bedroom door, drew my bath water as hot as I could stand it, and got out of my wrinkled clothes. I was about to step into the tub when I remembered the letter I had been writing before I had seen the lady in white. I went to the writing table, half afraid that I would find nothing. But there, behind the desk lamp, lay the crumpled paper where I had left it. The joy of my discovery was short lived, though, for I was again overcome with self-doubt and afraid to open the crumpled paper for fear that it would be blank.

I went back to the bathroom, slipped into the tub, and slowly and prayerfully opened the paper. My heart jumped when I found that it was exactly as I had remembered writing it! There was a description of my frightening encounter with the specter of Angus Harmer—ending mid-sentence—and the sketches of webs and spiders and the scroll-work design and the strange signatures of Julia Carter. Obviously I couldn't have written the letter in my sleep! This was evidence that my encounter with Angus Harmer hadn't been a dream. But I was suddenly appalled by the possibility that my subconscious might have taken possession of me, that my return to Harmer House was bringing back all the childhood experiences and fears I had repressed for nearly twenty years. I had first laid eyes on Angus Harmer in the library. Was the specter I saw the night before a twenty-year-old reflection of the past? If I had looked at myself in the mirror at that moment, or caught my reflection in the window, would I have encountered the reflection of a frightened six-year-old? Had I occupied this very room as a child in those dark days?

I looked again at the scroll-work. It was excellently drawn. And while my ability to copy likenesses is perhaps better than average, my conceptual ability and draftsmanship are far below the level displayed in the drawing. Indeed, it looked as though a professional artist had drawn it. Then there were the signatures. The handwriting was beautiful, most definitely not mine. This seemed more than ever to confirm my fear that my return had been a sensory one. The complexities were staggering. Had I been living in someone else's fantasy world for the past twelve hours? Had this Julia Carter taken possession of me? Was I suffering from what the psychiatrists call disassociated ideas of reference? And if I had crossed that thin line between fantasy and reality, how did I get back? Was I back for good, or was I doomed forever in my dreams to continue reliving that past twelve hours?

Harmer House had been the Eden from which I was banished for reasons a six-year-old couldn't understand. And the chilling possibility that I might continue to return to this dark Eden in fantasy during unguarded moments of sleep filled me with horror.

The scrap of paper I held in my hand was my only link with the real, tangible world. And except for the fact that it was material—something I could hold onto—it, too, was enigmatic. It served only to raise more questions when, for the sake of my sanity, I desperately needed answers. Though the prospects were frightful, I could somehow cope with the fact that I might be regressing mentally to a traumatic experience of my early childhood. But that still didn't account for the lady in white or for Edith's cryptic remark about my likeness to Julia—whoever she was.

My mental anguish was growing unbearable. I was torturing myself with questions, so I put the paper aside,

picked up a washcloth and soap, and began washing to occupy my hands and free my mind. In doing so, moments
later, I discovered that my problem, while no less com-
plex, wasn't entirely a mental one. My attention was
drawn to three small bruises on my right upper arm,
bruises I hadn't had the day before. They had been made
by strong fingers that had gripped my arm in a vise-like
hold—exactly as I had remembered Harold holding on to
me as he had led me upstairs shortly after I had seen
Angus Harmer in the library window!

Harold could claim that he had stayed in town, but his
presence in the house was evidenced by the bruises he left
on my arm. It was clear that Harold had lied to me. But
why?

After my bath, I dressed in a blue cotton pantsuit and
canvas shoes suitable for hiking through the countryside. I
longed to get out of the house and to talk to Mark private-
ly in an effort to enlist his aid in helping me solve my dilemma. And I hoped that he would have time to take a
walk with me after lunch.

I wasn't ready to face Harold or Edith alone, so I decided to wait in my room until lunch time. I stared out of
the window for a while, going over the previous night's
events and thinking that there was surely something more
than a scrap of paper and three bruises to indicate that my
night of horror had been something other than a nightmare
or, worse yet, evidence that I was going out of my mind—
or someone else's mind! The problem was convoluted,
though, and kept leading me back, maze-like, to our after-
dinner conversation, a conversation that both Harold and
Edith claimed never took place.

It was true that I remembered little about Harold's
leading me back upstairs after my encounter with the
ghost of Angus Harmer. But I most definitely remembered
entering the bedroom and the shock at realizing that he

hadn't replaced the lock on my door. That impression was very strong.

I turned from the window and looked at the lock again. It was a large bolt lock secured to the door several inches above the doorknob. I could see it clearly from across the room; it would have been impossible for me to have overlooked it. I went to the door to inspect it more closely. It appeared as though it had been there for years, but as I bent to study it, I thought I detected the faint odor of varnish or stain. I rubbed my fingers across it. It wasn't moist or sticky, but when I pressed my fingernail into the groove of one of the wood screws, it left a deep indentation, and a gummy substance stuck to my fingernail.

I tried to press my nail into the wood screws holding the door hinges, but the material in the grooves was hard. I noticed, too, that the stain on the bolt was lighter than that of the catch. Despite Harold's denial, the bolt had been recently replaced!

The discovery was made only seconds before I was startled by a sharp rapping on the door and Harold's call to me. I unlocked the door and opened it, averting Harold's eyes in the ridiculous notion that he would somehow see from my expression that I had discovered his deceit.

"Mr. Shorewood is here," he said. "Lunch will be served in a few minutes."

"Fine," I said, a little too loudly, I thought, in an effort to sound casual. "Please tell Mr. Shorewood that I'll be down in a moment."

I made a last-minute critical check in the mirror and ran a comb through my hair. Considering my lack of sleep, I didn't look too badly. I was thankful that I didn't look the way I felt—haggard and pale. It was a good feeling to know that Mark was in the house. I was very much dependent upon him now—particularly since he was the Harmers' attorney and had known them for years. If any-one could make sense of Harold's and Edith's actions, it would be Mark Shorewood. Then too, there was something very solid and trustworthy about him. Other than my foster father, I couldn't think of anyone in whom I would place more trust than Mark—nor anyone I would rather trust.

After freshening my makeup, I went downstairs. Harold was wheeling a serving cart down the hallway from the kitchen as I entered the dining room. Mark and Edith were seated at the table, apparently engaged in a serious and private discussion, for they were unsmiling, and broke off their conversation abruptly as I entered the room.

Edith was in her usual place at the far end of the table. Mark was seated to her left, and I saw that a place had been set for me across from Mark, on Edith's right. It was Edith who first saw me and, as though nothing had happened at breakfast, she gave me the same charming smile she had given me when I met her the day before in Mark's presence, a smile that seemed more for Mark's benefit than for mine.

"Here she is," Edith said in a high-pitched, light-hearted voice.

Mark rose and came around the table to shake hands with me. "Miss Gilmore," he said. "It's good to see you again."

"I've looked forward to our meeting again," I said. "But I thought we had decided on Elizabeth."

"Of course," Mark said, helping me with my chair. "Elizabeth it is."

Mark took his place across from me as Harold entered and began serving us. It troubled me that Mark seemed more distant than he had been on our first meeting. It wasn't just the formality of his calling me by my last name again. It was more than that. The instant rapport I had felt with him at our first meeting was no longer there. His actions towards me were most cordial, if not warm, but for some strange reason, I felt as though I was seated across the table from a complete stranger.

As Edith talked, I watched Mark closely. The day I met him, he had been dressed in a conservative business suit, but now he was casually dressed in slacks and a white, pullover turtle-neck sweater that made his hair appear much darker and his eyes even bluer. He was more handsome than I remembered, and I enjoyed looking at him. His face was most expressive, and I studied it as he reacted to Edith's remarks. Occasionally he'd glance my way, but each time he did, he'd see that I was looking at him, and he'd look quickly back to Edith again. This, too, I thought exceedingly strange. One of the mannerisms I had liked most about him was his confident gaze.

I was beginning to wonder if I wasn't being too critical of him, too unfair in my judgment. Maybe, I thought, I had expected too much of our second meeting. After all, I could hardly expect him to throw his arms around me and kiss me simply because we had established an easy rapport on our first meeting! Though I certainly wouldn't have minded had he done so. I suppose I was hurt because he had called me by my last name and because his actions weren't as warm towards me as I'd hoped they'd be. But even this was silly of me. I had talked to him for only an hour and had known him for only a day. It was absurd for me to expect his actions to correspond to my feelings for him, feelings which, I was discovering, were far deeper than I had realized.

I was still immersed in my thoughts when I noticed that the tone of Edith's voice had changed, ending on a questioning note. I looked up to see that she had directed the question to me.

"Don't you think so?" she repeated.

"I'm sorry," I said. "I didn't hear the question. My mind must have wandered for a moment."

Edith reached over and patted my hand sympathetically. "That's perfectly all right, my dear," she said, glancing knowingly at Mark. "We understand. I was just saying that the salad was very good, don't you think? The vegetables were picked fresh this morning from Harold's garden."

I was puzzled by Edith's comment and her knowing glance at Mark. But I let it pass in my astonishment that I had been so engrossed with my thoughts of Mark that I had eaten my salad without realizing it. Harold was already setting the main course before us.

"There's nothing like garden-fresh vegetables," I said to Edith, wishing that I had tasted them.

I had had nothing but a cup of coffee since dinner the evening before, and I was famished. I didn't mind at all when Edith continued to monopolize the conversation as I ate, asking Mark questions about events and people in town whom I didn't know. It wasn't until after we had finished eating and Harold had served coffee that Edith changed the topic of conversation to something I *did* know about—me. And it was only then that her earlier comment, her knowing glance at Mark, and Mark's cool attitude towards me began to make sense. I would never cease to be amazed at Edith's mercurial personality changes, and, judging from Mark's reaction, I could see that this was a facet of her personality new to him as well.

The change came when I remarked to Edith that the lunch had been delicious and that I had been extremely hungry. Edith seized the innocent remark and used it skilfully to guide the conversation in the direction she wanted it to go.

"I'm not at all surprised that you were hungry," she said. "You didn't touch a thing at breakfast."

Mark came into the conversation—quite innocently—at that point, as I'm sure Edith knew he would. "Miss Harmer tells me you weren't feeling well," he said. "I was sorry to hear that."

56

"Not feeling well?" I said. "I feel perfectly fine, except for a loss of sleep."

I didn't want to go into details about my harrowing experiences or my discovery of deceit in Edith's presence, so I let it go at that. But it became obvious that I had played into Edith's hands without going any further. She countered with a remark that left both Mark and myself embarrassed and momentarily speechless.

"Mr. Shorewood is being tactful," she said. "I didn't tell him that you weren't feeling well physically. I told him that your behavior here has led us to believe that you're mentally ill and in need of psychiatric attention."

She said it matter-of-factly, as though she were discussing someone who wasn't present. Mark was visibly upset at the candor of her remark, and I was first astounded, then angry. I understood why they had stopped talking when I entered the room and why Mark had seemed wary of me. She had told him that I was crazy!

I checked an impulse to present her with the evidence I had since uncovered that she and Harold were being less than truthful with me and that I was not imagining all that had gone on at Harmer House the night before. Edith would have denied all, anyway, and it would only have served to create a bad scene. I finally decided that I could play their game too, and I said, "I fail to see the humor in your remark."

"No humor was intended," Edith said.

"I've been emotionally upset, Miss Harmer—and justifiably so—but I would hardly call that grounds for judging me insane."

Edith looked at Mark and shook her head, as though resigned to the fact that my case was obviously hopeless.

"I would consider claiming to see the ghost of my dead brother and being attacked by a ghost with a knife and claiming to have awakened Harold twice when he wasn't even in the house something more than an emotional upset!" Edith said. "Not to mention attributing conversations to me that never took place, and that ridiculous nonsense about the lock on your door. We'll certainly accept the apology you offered, Miss Gilmore, but I don't think that your mental problem will improve by your pretending that it doesn't exist!"

It was apparent that Edith was a deceptive and articulate adversary. As the tension mounted in our exchange, I could see that Mark was ill at ease and restless. Obviously, no one wanted to witness such a scene. I had the feeling that he wanted to interrupt the conversation before it got out of hand, but that he wasn't quite sure that it was his business to do so. He stared into his coffee cup during most of the exchange, but glanced at me fleetingly to see my reaction when Edith had finished talking.

Edith was clearly trying to draw me out. She wanted me to recount my incredible experience before Mark. For some reason, she wanted Mark to think me insane! I had to think quickly. In a showdown before Mark, it would be my word against Edith's and Harold's. And my story was so fantastic, I could hardly believe it myself! How could I expect Mark to believe it? Particularly since he hardly knew me and, for all he knew about me, I really could be mentally ill! Edith was still looking at me, expecting me to defend myself. But I knew that this was neither the time nor the place to do so.

"You're right, Miss Harmer," I said. "One can't overcome problems by pretending that they don't exist. If you'd like, we'll talk about it later this afternoon. But there are always two sides, aren't there? I'm afraid that we're both much too emotional about it to discuss it after a fine meal."

"It's not *me* who's too emotional to talk about it," Edith said. "And when you accuse me of saying things that I didn't say, I think the least you can do is offer me an explanation—if you have one."

"I'd much prefer to take a walk right now," I said. "It's been a long time since I've seen the grounds—that is, if Mark will escort me so I don't get lost. I don't think I'd remember my way around any more."

"It would be my pleasure," Mark said, getting up from his chair. He was quite visibly relieved at being given the opportunity to quit the scene, and no doubt he felt some obligation to me for having been made a party to what should have been a personal and private conversation between Edith and myself.

"Are you trying to say that I've misrepresented your problem?" Edith asked as Mark came around the table to help me with my chair.

"Not at all. I'm simply saying that I'd prefer to take a walk, rather than discussing my problem so soon after lunch."

"If you'll excuse us, Miss Harmer?" Mark said.

Edith seemed surprised that Mark was so eager to leave, but she had little choice but to give in.

"Of course, Mr. Shorewood," she said.

I didn't look back as we left the dining room. There was no need to. I could feel the tension in the air and I knew that she was burning with anger. It hadn't gone according to her plan—that was evident. Whatever her plan was, I didn't like the role I had been assigned!

Chapter Seven

We walked in silence, deep in thought, for perhaps five or ten minutes, taking the pathway which lay a quarter of a mile or so from the house and which wound deeply into the woods towards the creek. The sky remained overcast and heavy dark clouds were still gathering. It hadn't rained for several hours, but the storm clouds were again closing in quickly. Once into the woods, however, one could only occasionally see the sky in patches above trees that had shed their leaves early. It occurred to me that I hadn't seen the sun since I had driven through Maryland on my way to Harmer House. And while I normally prefer rain to sunshine, I would have welcomed the sun to that dismal house.

The woods were lovely, deep and thick with autumn leaves on the branches overhead and on the ground. The leaves would have crackled nicely underfoot had it not been for the rain. But as it was, the sodden leaves didn't respond when we trod upon them, and this contributed to the majestic silence of the woods which now surrounded us, enveloped us, the elms and walnuts and oaks and maples reluctantly shedding their gold and crimson leaves in preparation for the dead of winter.

Mark delighted in watching the squirrels as they gathered walnuts, scampered up the trees, chasing one another in a last frolic before their hibernation. I enjoyed their antics, too. And being with Mark made me forget the sadness of autumn. Even as a child, when the teacher would have us gather brightly colored autumn leaves to paste on construction paper, or trace, or press, or whatever else we did with them, I was never fooled by nature's camouflage. Not that I looked upon them morbidly as being dead. I didn't. I looked upon them sadly as once having had life. I had always had a reverence for life—all life. And nature couldn't seduce me with her brilliant colors. Even as a child, I was never sure that spring would come again.

Despite the astonishing and unnerving scene with Edith, and despite my usual autumn sadness, the woods had a tranquilizing effect upon me. I was completely relaxed once we left sight of Harmer House, relaxed, that is, except for an occasional moment of apprehension when I wondered what Mark thought of me after Edith's revelations. I watched him closely, hoping for some outward sign of what he thought, but he was preoccupied by the panorama of Indian summer, and only once in a while did he glance my way and smile—a distantly friendly smile, nothing more. He had picked up a stick along the way and was using it for a cane as we walked, and we walked very slowly along the twisting, leaf-strewn pathway until we finally reached the creek.

"Would you like to sit down and rest?" he asked.

"If you'd like."

He took his raincoat off and spread it across the trunk of an old uprooted walnut tree that had fallen beside the creek. I sat down and looked out over the creek.

"The creek looks smaller than I remembered it," I said.

"*You* were smaller in those days," Mark suggested, sitting down beside me. "Do you remember this spot?"

"No, should I?"

"This was Angus' favorite fishing spot. That willow overhanging the creek provides shade and attracts the fish

61

in summer. The three of us fished here a few times. You don't remember that, do you?"

"The three of us?" I said, surprised. "You mean that we've gone fishing together?"

Mark laughed. "Well, not exactly *together*. How old were you that year?"

"Six."

"That would have made me ten years old," Mark said. "I hadn't discovered girls yet—didn't even acknowledge their existence. So I'm afraid I considered you an inter-loper—more of a tag-along than a fellow fisherman. You used to catch lots of fish and insist upon throwing them back again. I could never understand that at all. Then, too, there was a time or two that I didn't catch anything at all to speak of. That didn't exactly endear you to me either."

"I don't imagine so," I said, laughing. "Will you ever forgive me?"

"Maybe some day," Mark answered, smiling.

It was delightful talking to someone who remembered me from those days. "I wish I could remember," I said.

"You were awfully young. Those days impressed me because I considered you a definite threat to our fishing parties, and I could never understand why Angus insisted upon dragging you along."

"Do you remember anything else about me?"

"Very little, I'm afraid. I wouldn't have anything to do with you except when Angus made our fishing parties a threesome. I remembered that you talked all the time, and I was convinced that I didn't catch any fish because you scared them away with your big mouth. Of course, that didn't account for *your* catching so many, but it helped me rationalize my catching so few," Mark said, chuckling.

"I must have been terrible!"

"All girls are terrible to a ten-year-old fisherman."

"I guess that brings me full circle in twenty years," I said.

"Full circle?"

"I have a feeling that Edith considers me as much an interloper at Harmer House as you did."

"Oh, no," Mark said. "I'd find it hard to believe that Edith would think that."

"Do you find what she said of me at lunch hard to believe?"

Mark looked at me in surprise, realizing that I had brought to the surface what we had both been thinking about for the past half hour. "I'm quite bewildered," he said. "I really don't know *what* to think."

"You might think me innocent until proven guilty," I said.

"You've got a point. But you're assuming that I accept Edith's diagnosis. She's hardly qualified to make judgment on such matters. I think psychiatry is a little out of her field. Your explanation about being emotionally upset makes sense to me. Frankly, I'm shocked that Edith would say such things to your face."

"Maybe she had an ulterior motive."

Mark looked at me questioningly. "What would that be?"

"I don't know. I'm just casting around for motivations."

"Well it's not like her at all," Mark observed.

"Isn't it? How well do you really know Edith?"

"My father was the Harmer attorney until he died," Mark said. "I've known her for about twenty years, I guess. Not as well as I knew Angus, of course. Edith was always rather cool—perhaps *distant* would be a better description. She's been much friendlier since her brother's death. I suppose that's because my business is with *her* now, and I deal with her more."

"Did she tell you about the lock on my door?"

"Only that you said there wasn't one, and she says there is one."

"Yes, there *is* a lock on my door, but it was put there

sometime this morning. The stain and varnish are dry, but fresh. You can smell them! Yet Harold claims that the lock has been there for years!"

"Maybe it *is* a new lock and it's slipped his mind. He's getting pretty old, you know. Some people are forgetful when they get old."

"But I'm telling you, the lock *wasn't* on my door last night. Surely he wouldn't forget that he replaced it this morning!"

"Even so, the lock has no bearing on your nightmare, or whatever it was, does it?"

"Not a direct bearing, no," I admitted. "But do you have any idea how a woman—alone and in a strange house with strange people—feels when she can't lock the door to her room?"

"You'd probably feel insecure."

"In a place like Harmer House, *terrified* is a more fitting description. And if one wanted to drive a strange woman from the house, I couldn't think of a better way to start."

"Surely you don't think Edith is trying to drive you from the house?"

"I don't know what to think," I said. "Before I came here, I didn't think that I'd be seeing ghosts, either! Do you believe in ghosts, Mark?"

"Ghosts? I can't say that I do believe in them. I've never really thought about it. I've never seen one, but there exist lots of things I haven't seen, and the older I get, the more inclined I become not to disbelieve in anything. We have our share of ghosts in town, you know. Mostly in the older houses built before the Civil War."

"Do you know any reliable people who have seen them?"

"Sure. Several. The high school principal lives in a house that he claims is haunted. He sees the ghost frequently."

64

"Then you wouldn't think me mentally ill if I told you that I *did* see the ghost of Angus Harmer and the ghost of a woman last night?"

Mark paused, considering the question, then spoke with deliberation, choosing his words carefully. "No," he said. "I wouldn't think you're mentally ill for thinking you saw ghosts. But since Edith and Harold live in the house all the time and have never seen them, I wouldn't rule out the possibility that what you saw was imagined. After all, lots of people see things which—they later learn—weren't at all what they thought they were."

"But Edith and Harold are the ones who told me about the ghosts in the first place!"

Mark sighed. "Elizabeth," he said, "Edith claims that she never mentioned ghosts to you and that she doesn't know what you're talking about. And Harold concurs. What can I say? That's what makes me all the more sure that you either had a very bad and vivid nightmare, or that you simply imagined that you saw them. As you said, it's a strange house to you, and if you were up last night with the lightning in a house full of strange shadows, it would be perfectly reasonable that you'd be frightened and that the strange shadows might have appeared to be other than what they really were."

"But I've got a letter I wrote in the middle of the night describing how I saw Angus Harmer's ghost," I said. "One doesn't get up in the middle of a nightmare, write down the details, then resume the nightmare! And as for Harold's denial of the ghost conversation, he denies being in the house last night, too. But he was there. He said that he stayed in town playing cards with his relatives, but after I saw Angus Harmer in the library window, Harold took me up to my room. I've got bruises on my arm where he gripped it tightly because of my hysteria. No one else has gripped my arm like that. And I'd like to know how he bruised my arm if he wasn't in the house!"

"Both Harold and his brother-in-law play poker in town with several other men every Friday night," Mark said. "They usually play so late that Harold stays at his brother-in-law's. I saw him in town last night myself. And as for your bruises, I'm sure there's a reasonable explanation for them."

I was hurt that Mark was taking Edith's part. I suppose I really shouldn't have been. Had he told me a similar story, I too probably would have thought there was a more rational explanation. I probably wouldn't have been as candid in telling him so as he had been with me, though. He was trying to ease my mind, but the more we talked, the more angry I became with Edith for lying, and the more hurt I became that Mark wouldn't accept my version of the incidents that had taken place.

Although I tried to hold them back, the tears welled in my eyes. I felt alone again, even with Mark beside me. I had hoped for more sympathy from him, more understanding and concern. I tried to brush the tears away nonchalantly, but Mark saw me doing so.

"Hey," he said, putting his arm around me, "there's no cause for tears."

He handed me his handkerchief, and I blotted the tears away. "I'm being silly, I guess," I said. "But I had hoped you'd be more concerned—that you'd be on my side."

Mark turned me toward him, looking into my eyes. "I *am* on your side, Elizabeth," he said. "Believe me."

"What would happen if I just packed up and went back to New York, refusing the inheritance?" I said, handing him back his handkerchief.

"If you refused the inheritance, it would eventually go to Edith as next of kin. But you're not thinking of doing that, are you?"

"No. Not yet, anyway. I was just asking."

"I should hope not. Angus really wanted you to have the inheritance, you know."

"Yes, I know. But what if I were judged insane or incompetent? What would happen to the estate then?"

"Well, since the terms of the inheritance call for administering to the house, and if you were unable to care for it, Edith could contest the will. But Elizabeth! Surely you're not suggesting—"

"I really don't know what I'm suggesting," I interrupted. "I don't know. Maybe Edith really believes that I'm mentally ill!"

"No," Mark said. "I think she was just overwrought. It's probably the strain of her brother's death, and having to face leaving Harmer House. It's the only place she's known for thirty years."

"Then maybe she should stay, if it really means that much to her. I don't want to be responsible for driving her out of her own house."

"I assure you, she doesn't want to stay. She's told me so herself. She's too old to rattle around in that great, drafty hulk of a place, and she knows it. But that doesn't make it any easier for her to leave. She'd move to Richmond even if the place remained hers."

As Mark spoke, we could hear the snapping sound of large raindrops hitting the leaves above us, and could see the rippling rings made by the widely scattered drops hitting the surface of the water in the creek.

"I guess we'd better be heading back to the house," he said. "Looks like we're in for another downpour."

We walked along the path towards the house as silently as we had come. The more I thought about it, the more convinced I became that while Edith may have had other motivations as well, she was denying the existence of the ghosts to discredit me. She was certainly making me seem foolish in Mark's eyes. And I couldn't simply leave the house and let Mark go on thinking forever that I had let my imagination run wild, like a child frightened from having seen a horror movie. Much as I would like to have walked away from Harmer House that very moment, I didn't like being thought silly enough to believe something I had imagined. I needed a witness—particularly to Harold's participation—if for no other purpose than to restore some semblance of dignity to myself in Mark's eyes. Circumstances had made me appear a simpering, suspicious and naive six-year-old!

I wanted Mark to see for himself what was going on at Harmer House, but it was clear that if his presence were known, neither Edith nor Harold would be quite so obviously deceitful. The best way to avoid that would be to sneak Mark into the house after Edith and Harold had retired. That is, if I could get Mark's co-operation.

I was considering how best to approach him with the idea so that the suggestion wouldn't sound absurd, when he said: "Do you still want to move into the hotel for the rest of the weekend, Elizabeth?"

"No," I said, "I've changed my mind. I've never run away from anything before, and I have no intention of starting now."

"Good for you," Mark reassured me. "Things will work out fine, you'll see. I'm sure that the emotional strain of coming back here after all these years and being confronted with symbols of your past have affected your nervous system more than you realize."

"Perhaps you're right," I said, thinking that I could prove otherwise to him if given the chance. But in view of his defense of Edith, I wondered if he would help me—if he would really care to. For all I knew, he was still being tactful with me. Maybe he still thought that there was some truth to Edith's remarks, and that he was truly helping me by showing kindness and consideration. He really didn't know me that well. It was a terrible, nagging doubt that was eased somewhat by his next words.

"How about dinner tonight? We could go to a movie afterwards, if you'd like. It would do you good to get away from the place for an evening, and it would give the town gossips something to talk about, my escorting a beautiful redhead around town. We don't often get strangers in Blackston, you know. It would contribute to my stature enormously. There aren't many people who know strangers—even in New York."

I laughed. "I'd be delighted," I said. "That sounds like a most worthy cause."

Mark looked at his watch. "I've got a couple of appointments, but I can make it back here by six. That okay with you?"

"Fine," I said, thinking that our date would be most opportune. It would give Mark a chance to get to know me better and perhaps realize that I was too level-headed to be taken in by nightmares or flights of fancy, and it would give me a chance to approach him with my plan to sneak him into the house. And returning late from a date would give us a good opportunity to do so.

The rain came down harder, but sheltered by the trees we continued to walk slowly. I slipped once, nearly falling. Mark grabbed my hand to help me regain my balance, and continued holding it as we walked. I felt much better. The prospect of a night out pleased me, not only because it would give me an opportunity to get away from the house, but because it meant that Mark was interested in me. He wouldn't have gone to the trouble of asking me out on a date simply to ease my mind about the goings-on at Harmer House. And now, walking along with my hand in his, I didn't feel alone.

"Do you know Julia Carter?" I asked him.

The question surprised him, and for an instant, he almost stopped walking. "Julia Carter?" he said. "Why do you ask?"

"Edith compared me to her. I thought you might know who she is."

"She compared *you* to Julia?"

"Yes. Who is she?"

"She was Edith's daughter."

"Was?"

"Yes. She died a long time ago," Mark said. "It must have been about a year or so before you came to Harmer House. Angus thought the world of her. She was really more of a daughter to him than a niece. I think that's one of the reasons he wanted to adopt you so badly. Julia's death left a void in him that was never filled."

"I didn't even know that Edith had a daughter. How did she die?"

"Why do you ask?" Mark's tone of voice was sharp, and his hand tightened on mine from tension. It was the first time he had spoken harshly to me, and it hurt me.

"I just wondered, that's all," I said. "If she was Edith's daughter, and she died that long ago, she couldn't have been very old. . . ."

"I'm sorry, Elizabeth," Mark said, squeezing my hand, the warmth in his voice returning. "I didn't mean to snap at you. It's just that, under the circumstances, I didn't want to discuss her death, that's all."

"What do you mean, *under the circumstances?*"

Mark smiled, but the smile faded quickly. "You'd have made a good trial attorney," he said. "You certainly do press on relentlessly."

"Objection overruled," I said. "You're evading the question."

"I meant that I thought a discussion of Julia's death might upset you. And I don't want to upset you."

"I don't think that I could be more upset than I have been," I said. "I'd like to know about her—particularly since Edith compared me to her. You make her sound very mysterious."

"Not mysterious, just . . . well, strange. She was very young—just over twenty, I think—and I guess it's natural to ask about the cause of death in one so young." Mark paused, then finally added, "She committed suicide."

"That's terrible! Why? Do they know?"

"No. She left no note or anything. There was no apparent reason. In fact, she had every reason not to, I think. She was to be married the following day. "If her impending marriage had anything to do with it, it was never discovered. It's not a very pleasant subject. That's why I was hesitant about telling you."

"I'm beginning to wonder if there's *anything* about the Harmers and Harmer House that's pleasant," I said.

"Those things happen."

"What happened to her father—Edith's husband?"

"I don't know for sure," Mark said. "I guess he's still alive. Lives in the Midwest somewhere. He and Edith were divorced, I think."

"I wonder why I remind Edith of Julia?"

"Maybe you resemble her, or have similar mannerisms."

"It seems to me that it was after I'd told her that I'd seen the ghosts that she compared me to her."

"I don't know," Mark said. "I know little about Julia."

"Did you know her at all?"

"Not really. I saw her a few times the first summer I came out to fish with Angus and my dad. I must have been eight or nine, I think. I don't remember her, though. I can't picture her at all. I just remember a young woman being around once in a while, that's all."

We left the protective shelter of the woods and hurried across the grounds to get in out of the rain. I asked Mark to check my car for me, and we got into it. The battery was low, but it started immediately, and Mark let the engine run for a few minutes to charge the battery. Then, realizing that he was late for his appointment in town, he told me he would pick me up at six, and asked me to say goodbye to Edith for him.

I watched him drive off, and I was still thinking about Julia as I walked to the house, when it struck me what Mark had said about Julia's suicide and her impending marriage.

The lady in white wore a bridal gown and carried a knife! A chill ran through me as I remembered the blood-like stain on the gown, and I wondered if Julia Carter had committed suicide with a knife!

Chapter Eight

It was not the least pleasant entering the house again alone. I tried to push the thoughts of Julia from my mind with the delightful prospect of the evening in town with Mark that lay before me. But still my muscles tensed involuntarily as I entered the house and closed the door behind me.

The damp and musty odor of the house hung heavily in the dark and forbidding interior of the entrance hall, and it was even more obvious and repugnant to me after the clean, fresh air of the woods. I looked around as I removed my rain boots, ill at ease with the ever-present feeling of being watched. The place was tomblike, quiet and clammy and cloistered in impenetrable shadows which seemed to absorb what little light the stained glass windows allowed.

I looked into the shadows of the second floor as I removed my raincoat, and I had misgivings about my decision to stay. Certainly I wouldn't spend another night alone in the place! If I couldn't get Mark to go along with my plan, then I'd stay in town. But I knew that Mark would help me now. He might not think the idea of sneaking into the house a good one, but I knew I could convince him of its importance to me. And he would help.

I simply had to discover what was going on at Harmer House. Was the lady in white real—someone living in the house whom I didn't know about? Or was she indeed a ghost—the ghost of Edith's daughter, Julia Carter? And why did Edith and Harold tell me about the ghosts, then deny that they had done so? Was it because they had had second thoughts and didn't want me to tell Mark about the ghosts?

No, I thought, I couldn't just leave the house with these questions unanswered—particularly when Edith had used them to discredit me in front of Mark. I truly didn't want the inheritance. I'd gladly have left the Harmer House in the care of its ghosts.

The dining room was now empty, but I saw light coming from the library and found Edith there, by the fireplace, alone and reading. She marked her place in the book with her index finger and looked up as I entered.

"I see you got caught in the rain," she said, smiling, her eyes darting to me, then to the door, then back to me again. "Where's Mr. Shorewood?"

"He had to hurry back for an appointment. He asked me to say goodbye for him."

Learning that Mark wasn't behind me, she changed her manner completely. "I see," she said coolly, focusing her attention on the book again.

I waited for a moment to see if she'd look up, but she ignored me as though I had left the room.

"I won't be dining with you tonight," I said. "Mr. Shorewood is taking me to dinner in town."

She looked up again, arching one eyebrow in surprise as though wondering why on earth anyone would want to be seen in my company.

"Then I take it that you've decided not to leave us yet?" she said.

"I've decided to stay until Monday, as I had planned. That is, if you don't mind."

"Certainly not," she said. "This will soon be your house. But I trust that you'll have enough consideration to spare us the details of your hallucinations!"

She looked at me in a rather amused fashion as she said it. She quite obviously enjoyed toying with me, and it made me angry. I nearly told her that I trusted I would get to the bottom of what she called my hallucinations, but decided that it would be better if I let her think that I was letting the matter drop.

"I'm sure we won't have that problem again," I said.

"Good. Did you discuss our luncheon conversation with Mr. Shorewood?"

"Yes."

"And what did he think?"

"He thinks that my coming back to the place of my father's death after all these years was a traumatic shock and a great strain on me."

"I'm sure it is," Edith said. "And what do you think of Mr. Shorewood's evaluation?"

"I can find no other reasonable explanation," I said in truth.

"I only hope for your sake that it's as simple as that, Miss Gilmore."

"What do you mean?"

"I mean that I hope it's a simple, momentary problem, and not symptomatic of a more serious condition."

"And you think it might be more serious?"

"I don't know," Edith said.

"Like Julia's condition, perhaps?"

I was probing blindly, but I hit a nerve. Edith snapped upright and her eyes narrowed as an expression of pure hate came across her face.

"What do you know of Julia?" she snapped.

"I know very little about her."

"You have a bad habit of picking at old wounds, Miss Gilmore! I should think that the tragedy in your past would make you more sensitive to tragedy in the lives of others. You may be inheriting the Harmer House, but that doesn't give you license to constantly remind me of the Harmer tragedies."

"It was you who first mentioned Julia and compared me to her. If you're going to make such comparisons and make accusations about me before others, I think I too have a right to expect an explanation."

"Comparisons?"

"Yes. When you said that I was just like Julia!"

Edith looked at me with disdain. "More hallucinations, Miss Gilmore?" she said. "I thought you just assured me that we wouldn't have that problem again."

I could see that Edith was going to deny still another of our conversations. Curiously enough, I found solace in this one. If I had doubts about our conversation the previous evening, I certainly had no doubt about the subject we had discussed at the breakfast table. Since I hadn't slept since that conversation, no one could convince me that I had dreamed it! I was beginning to think that maybe Edith was becoming senile, forgetting things that she had said. At least she didn't deny the existence of Julia.

"Perhaps I misunderstood you at breakfast," I said. "I meant no harm."

Edith settled back in her chair, her anger subsiding. "I want you to keep your observations about my family to yourself," she said.

"Yes, of course. It won't happen again."

"Did you discuss Julia with Mr. Shorewood?"

"I asked him if he knew her. When I thought you had compared me to her, I was curious to know who she was."

"And what did Mr. Shorewood tell you?"

"That she was your daughter."

"Nothing more?"

"He said that she . . . died."

"Yes, she's *dead!*" Edith said sharply. "Did Mr. Shorewood tell you how she died?"

I hesitated, not wanting to answer the question. I wondered what Edith was up to. "As you suggested, Miss Harmer, I'd just as soon not discuss your family," I said.

"You're a bit late in making that decision. You've made it your business to discuss my family—you've gone out of your way to do so, in fact."

"Not intentionally," I said.

"I see only actions, not intentions," Edith observed sarcastically. "Didn't Mr. Shorewood tell you that Julia committed suicide?"

"He mentioned it."

"Yes, of course he did!" Edith said vehemently. "And I suppose he told you how she did it."

She fixed me with her dark eyes. She was unmerciful and relentless in her interrogation of me, and I wished that I hadn't let myself be drawn into the conversation. There was quite obviously a point to it which she had yet to thrust at me, and I dreaded the deadly way she was taking aim. "No," I said. "Mark didn't go into the details of her death, and I didn't ask."

"Well! That was an oversight on your part, *wasn't* it?"

"No, it wasn't. I was just curious about *who* she was, not how. . . ."

"She killed herself with a knife!" Edith interrupted. "Held the point to her heart and fell upon it! Does that please you, Miss Gilmore?"

I was stunned. "Please me?"

"Yes. You've made a habit of poking your nose into the

76

misfortunes of others. Now you know the whole story—
that should please you, I think."

"That's a monstrous thing to say, Miss Harmer! No, it
doesn't please me! And you're unjust to even think that it
would. Surely you can't possibly believe that I would take
pleasure in the details of your daughter's death."

"Can't I?" Edith said.

There was no use in arguing with her. Her suspicions
were boundless, and no matter what incident or conversation I could offer in my defense, she would strike it down
as never having taken place. Since there was no alternative, I decided to let her think what she liked, and to with-
draw from the conversation.

"I'll be in my room when Mr. Shorewood calls for me,"
I said. "I'd like to take a couple of books up with me, if
you don't mind."

Edith didn't reply. She turned her attention to her book
and took no further notice of me as I moved around the
room, selecting books from the shelves to take upstairs.
Had it not been for the fact Mark would soon be around
to help me, I would have left the house that very moment.
Edith's disclosure of Julia's horrible death confirmed my
worst suspicions about the lady in white. And my skin
crawled as I recalled her standing on the staircase landing
above me, her knife raised, the lightning flashing. I wanted
no more part of her—didn't even want to think of her, if I
could help it.

I looked over at Edith, and whatever animosity I had
for her left me as I watched her, a small, old woman in
mourning clothes, sitting hunched over a book, mourning,
no doubt, the passing of the entire Harmer family. She was
completely alone now. Old and awaiting death herself. It
was no wonder that she was strange and inscrutable and
preoccupied with death. These were suitable character-
istics for one who dwelled in the shadows of Harmer
House.

I wondered if it was possible that Angus Harmer, too, had committed suicide. It seemed impossible for him to have fallen accidentally over such a high railing. Mark knew about Julia's suicide. Perhaps that's why he seemed so troubled over Angus Harmer's death.

The rest of the afternoon was pleasant. I remained in my room reading by the fireplace and thoroughly enjoying the diversion. The storm had commenced again, and in daylight I found pleasure in the sound of the rain buffeting my window as I read in the warmth of the fire. I was so engrossed with my reading, in fact, that I didn't once think of the things that had plagued me since coming to the house.

At five I began dressing for my date with Mark, and it was about a quarter to six when I decided to wait for him downstairs. I was at the top of the staircase, about to descend, when I noticed Harold below me, at the door, talking to someone. I couldn't tell who it was from my angle, nor could I hear what was being said, but I assumed that it was Mark.

I went quickly down the stairs, but before I could reach the bottom step, Harold had closed the door and was standing in front of it, looking up at me. "Who was that?" I asked him.

"No one," Harold said.

"I heard you talking to someone, and I thought that it might have been Mr. Shorewood. He's supposed to be picking me up any minute now."

"I meant, no one you would know," Harold said, as I approached him. "It was a neighbor. Lives on a farm nearby."

"I see. I'm going to wait for Mr. Shorewood in the living room. Please let me know when he arrives."

"I will," Harold said.

The living room was dark. I turned on a lamp next to

an occasional chair and sat down to wait. There was nothing to do to pass the time. I had noticed when I first arrived that there wasn't a single television set or radio or phonograph in the entire house. And I realized while waiting that there were no newspapers or magazines either. Not one. Except for the cook, who came in from town every day, Harmer House was completely insulated from the outside world. I've often thought that getting away from the constant bombardment of news, occasionally, was good for a person's mind, but at Harmer House this seemed a way of life. One had little choice but to live in the past. I occupied my mind while waiting by thinking of Mark. Even so, the time dragged.

It was six twenty when I finally got so restless that I began pacing the floor in my anxiety to get out of the house. But I have never been good at floor pacing, so I decided instead to see if the library was occupied. I had just passed the dining room when I became aware of voices—those of Edith and Harold. The high-domed entry way and marble floor amplified the sound. I couldn't distinguish what was being said, but from the rising and falling tones and the rapidity of their words there was no doubt in my mind that they were arguing. I realized that their voices were coming from behind the closed library door, so I went back to the living room to pace awhile longer.

After a while, when I could no longer hear them arguing, Harold walked down the hallway past the living room without looking in. A minute or two later, Edith entered the living room. I braced myself for another episode with her, but to my surprise, she was in good spirits and gave no outward sign that she had been arguing. Indeed, I was to be witness to another of her mercurial mood changes. She seemed to have forgotten—or was simply disregarding—our earlier conflict, and she was genuinely cordial towards me. I came to the conclusion that, no matter how hard I tried, I would never understand her.

"I see Mr. Shorewood hasn't arrived yet," she said with an expression of concern, drawing her wheel chair opposite me.

"No. He was probably detained with one of his late appointments."

"Well, I wouldn't worry about him," Edith said as Harold wheeled the serving cart into the room. "Mr. Shorewood is very conscientious. He'll be here shortly, I'm sure. I had Harold make some hot chocolate. You'll join me, won't you?"

"Yes, thank you," I said.

Harold wheeled the serving tray between us and filled two cups, handing one to each of us. "I'll be going into town with the cook to get the car," he said. "Will there be anything else?"

"No, I don't think so," Edith said. "Will you be returning tonight?"

"No. I plan to stay in town again tonight."

"Very well," Edith said.

Harold left, and Edith kept me company while I waited for Mark. And she was surprisingly good company, too. She was curious about my life in New York, and talked at length about her life at Harmer House, telling me that she hadn't visited nearby Blackston in almost six years, mostly because Blackston was an old city, built during the days when there was danger of the shops flooding with mud from the streets during the rainy season. Consequently, the downtown section was fraught with intimidating high curbs and high steps leading to the older shops, making it nearly impossible for a person confined to a wheel chair to get around. I concluded that Edith wasn't a recluse by choice only. I could imagine the frustration of being confined to a wheel chair—especially in the country. She couldn't get out into the woods, and except for the sidewalk leading from the cobblestone drive to the house there were few places she could negotiate. Our conversation made me realize how small and restricted her world was. And it seemed to me that Richmond should be a welcome change for her, but I didn't tell her so.

She waited a long time with me, but finally grew tired and excused herself. I was surprised to discover that it was eight thirty. And though I hated to admit it, it seemed clear that Mark had no intention of picking me up.

At nine, I decided to go into town alone with the intention of taking a room at the hotel. Perhaps, I thought, I would look up Mark's phone number and call him in the morning. But on second thought I decided not to. There was the possibility that he had made our date only to ease out of the scene gracefully. And I again wondered if he believed Edith. It seemed to me that his not showing up was evidence that he did. Had he intended to make it and found, for some reason, that he couldn't, he surely would have sent word. If that was the case, then there would be little point in my trying to enlist his aid, and I thought I might just as well return for my things in the morning, tell Edith that I was refusing the inheritance, and go back to New York.

I wasted no time in changing my clothes, packing an overnight case, and getting out of the house. It was not only pouring rain, but the wind had come up, a cold buffeting wind that was whipping the rain into a mist that seemed to be penetrating everything—including my convertible. The cloudy sky had blocked out the moon, and it was pitch black.

When I closed the front door behind me, I had to wait on the porch for my eyes to become accustomed to the darkness. At first I couldn't even see my car, and I was frightened as I recalled what Harold had said about the bad dirt roads. But I knew that I'd be safer driving the nearly impassable roads the twenty miles or so to Blackston, than I'd be if I spent another night in Harmer House alone.

Even when my eyes had adjusted, the rain was so heavy that I could barely make out the car's silhouette. My teeth were chattering from the cold and dampness when I threw my overnight case in the back seat, got into the car and locked the doors from the inside. The vinyl seats were cold and clammy from the dampness, and I was eager to get the car started and the heater on. I turned on the ignition and pushed the starter button. The starter chattered, but the engine failed to ignite. I tried it again and again, but realized that, like the previous night, the engine wasn't going to start! The battery was still weak. It was only a matter of seconds until the starter began turning slower and slower, finally grinding to a stop. I waited prayerfully for a minute or two, then tried again, but when I pushed the starter button, nothing happened.

Despair settled over me like the cold, wet mist outside. I rested my forehead on the steering wheel and cried harder than I had ever cried in my life, the sobs shaking my body uncontrollably.

It seemed incredible to me that so much misfortune could befall me in such a short period of time. I simply wasn't geared for the emotional assault. I went through a number of states, from the depths of despair, a sort of emotional and physical numbness when I no longer cared what happened to me and considered going back into the house to let its inhabitants—living and dead—do their worst, to increasing degrees of physical and emotional discomfort and hence an awareness that made me again mindful and afraid of the dangers the house held for me.

I began considering my alternatives. There were really only two: I could go back into the house or I could spend the night in the car. The latter seemed to me the most intelligent option. I felt safe in the car, locked in. I got into the back seat and tried to get comfortable. But with the high wind and the drafty convertible, it was only a matter of minutes before I realized that I would catch pneumonia dressed only in my pantsuit and plastic raincoat. I was shivering painfully already and would probably be blue with cold in an hour or so.

What I needed was my coat and a blanket or two. I wouldn't make it through the night without them. And though I dreaded the idea of going back into the house even for the few minutes it would take me to get blankets and my coat, this was far better than being eventually forced into the house permanently from overexposure. Whether I liked it or not, I had to return to my room.

Gusty winds chilled me even more as I got out of the car and ran over the cobblestones to the sidewalk. The winds whipped the branches of the trees nearby into an awesome frenzy and a terrifying, whispering sound that chilled me even more than the cold and quickened my step. I climbed the front steps and was reaching for the door handle when I thought I heard someone call my name in a moaning voice a pitch or two lower than the occasional howls of the wind-buffeted trees. I looked toward the west end of the porch, the direction from which I thought the sound had come, but gave the porch and bushes only a fleeting glance when I realized that it must have been the wind I had heard.

I grabbed the door handle and pushed my shoulder against the door, anxious to get out of the wind and cold. But the handle didn't give. The door was locked! The night latch had apparently been set, and I had locked myself out!

"Elizabeth?"

The voice came from somewhere behind me. A masculine voice, low and rasping. It wasn't the wind. I spun around, startled, and strained my eyes trying to see into the shadows.

"Who's there?" I called.

There was no answer. No movement. I turned to the

door again, not believing that it was locked, and tried the door handle. But it was no use.

"Elizabeth?"

The voice was louder, nearer, harsher than before. This time, when I turned, I saw a figure moving from the shadow of the bushes at the west end of the porch. Whoever it was, he was moving towards me—most definitely a man.

"Who are you?" I said.

The man continued moving toward the porch steps without answering me.

"Who are you?" I screamed. "What do you want?"

Still there was no answer, and I turned back to the door, ringing the doorbell repeatedly and hammering on the door with my fists. "Edith!" I shouted. And I heard my own voice echoing from the woods: *Edith! Edith!* And the low laughter of the man behind me, and the scraping sound of his foot on the first porch step!

I turned around and backed against the door, kicking against it with my heel. "Edith! Open the door, *please.*"

The man climbed the steps, slowly, and raised his arm, his hand open and grasping, as though he intended to grab me by the throat!

"Who *are* you?" I screamed at him.

Are you? Are you? the woods repeated.

I heard only the man's laughter as my muscles convulsed from fear, and I began to pitch forward as I lost my sense of balance, then jerked back violently, thudding against the door. I remember screaming at the top of my lungs, and my knees buckling as I reached back to the door handle for support.

The last thing I remember was the man coming closer and closer and the feeling of my hand sliding down the surface of the door, grasping for something to hold on to as I fell and tumbled endlessly into blackness.

Chapter Nine

I tried to sink deeper into the funnel of warm, protective darkness away from the cold and from fear. But light kept flickering into my consciousness, growing in intensity. I moved my head back to avoid the light, but it persisted and I finally blinked my eyes into focus and found that I was staring into a fireplace. I lay motionless for a long time, completely relaxed and sinking into the darkness again until my mind gathered fragments of thought and I realized what had brought about the darkness. I sat bolt upright, my heart pounding wildly.

Dizziness and nausea overcame me. I looked around, but things swam, distorted and wave-like, making me fall back again. The images registered on my stunned brain: a bed, a wall, an open door, the man on the porch—all moved before my eyes with equal clarity, along with frames of blackness, until I made a conscious effort to clear my head and to focus on the present. It was then that I realized I was on a sofa in my bedroom at Harmer House!

I sat up again, leaning against the back of the sofa for support. And as my head cleared more, I remembered the details of my confrontation with the man on the porch. I looked down at my clothes, shocked to see that I was wearing neither raincoat nor boots! Had I lain down on the sofa and fallen asleep waiting for Mark? Had I merely dreamed of trying to start the car and of encountering the man?

I got to my feet and looked around. Except for my bedroom door, which was standing open, the room was exactly as I had left it. I looked at my watch. It was nine forty-five. I recalled having hot chocolate with Edith, then coming up to my room to change. Could I have come upstairs and, after changing, lain down for a moment and fallen asleep? No, I thought, that was impossible. But how then had I gotten back to my room?

I left the room, walked down the hallway to the top of the stairs and looked down. The entry way was dark except for a splotch of light before the door to the library. I hurried down the stairs and crossed the marbled floor. As I did so, I noticed that my boots were exactly where I had left them after my walk with Mark. My God! I thought. Is Edith right? Is this cursed house affecting my mind?

When I entered the library, I found Edith reading by the fire in the same spot I had found her earlier in the afternoon. She jumped, startled, as I entered the room, dropping the book she was reading to her lap.

"I'm sorry," I said. "I didn't mean to frighten you."

"I thought you had gone to bed," Edith said. "Don't tell me you're still waiting for Mr. Shorewood?"

"No, I'm not. I just happened to notice the light. I thought you had retired."

"I decided to read for a while. You *have* been sleeping," she said, looking at me closely. "I'll bet you woke up hungry. You haven't eaten since lunch."

I didn't want to give Edith the opportunity of accusing me of further fantasies, so I broached the subject obliquely. "I thought I heard the doorbell and someone pounding on the door," I said. "Did you hear anything?"

"The door? No. I certainly would have heard had anyone been at the door. I've been here since dinner."

"Perhaps it was a loose shutter in the wind," I said.

"Why don't you fix yourself something to eat. I'd have had Harold bring you up a tray if I'd known that Mr. Shorewood wasn't going to be here. But Harold's in town, now."

"Yes, I know," I said. "I was in the living room when he left."

"Oh?" Edith said. "Why didn't you let me know. I would have kept you company while you were waiting."

I wasn't surprised by Edith's remark. I had grown accustomed to her denying all incidents and conversations to which Mark wasn't a party. And I didn't give her the pleasure of questioning my sanity on this occasion either. "I didn't know you were in the library," I said.

"Well, no matter," she said, putting her book down on the table beside her and looking at the clock. "It's ten o'clock. I think I'll retire now. Will you be using the library tonight?"

"No. I have a couple of books in my room. I think I'll fix myself some tea and go to bed too."

Edith turned off the library lights and followed me out, bidding me good night. I watched her cross the entryway to her room, then I went along the west corridor towards the kitchen. On the way, I stopped by the living room and switched on a light. The serving tray was where Harold had left it, and Edith had made a point of emphasizing that she had been in the library since dinner and that she would have kept me company had she known that I was in the living room. Yet here was the evidence to the contrary. I switched the light off and went to the kitchen to fix myself some tea and toast.

I no longer tried to figure out whether Edith was doing these things to me deliberately, or whether she was simply losing her memory. Her behavior was simply irrational, beyond comprehension—as was almost everything else that was happening to me at Harmer House. But had she been in the library all evening—as she claimed—she would have heard me banging on the door and ringing the bell. And how could I have gotten to my room without her knowing it?

It was at that moment that I thought of looking for my raincoat. As nearly as I could figure, it hadn't been more than half an hour from the time I had fainted on the porch until I awoke in my room. If someone had brought me up to my room and had taken off my raincoat, it had to be somewhere in the room. And there was a good chance that it would still be wet.

I made my tea and toast, put them on a tray and decided to take the service stairs to my room. The stairs were extremely narrow and rose sharply halfway up between floors to a landing before veering to the right. I could find no light switch at the foot of the stairs, and the light from the kitchen barely illuminated the first dozen steps. I left the kitchen light on and, after a moment's hesitation, I began climbing the steps. Only the fact that it was the shortest route to my room and enabled me to avoid the dimly lit front of the house gave me the courage I needed to begin my ascent into the darkness.

The old steps groaned underfoot as I climbed. I was nearly to the first landing when my courage began to fail me. The passage was so narrow that I was blocking off the little light that penetrated the darkness from the kitchen. And this, coupled with the eerie groaning of the steps, was beginning to unnerve me. I had climbed far enough to see that the passage beyond the bend also lay in inky darkness. And at the very moment I made this observation, the step beneath my foot groaned very loudly, sending a shock through my nervous system.

After hesitating for a moment to catch my breath, I decided to go back down the stairs and to take the front stairway to my room. There was little point, I thought, in straining my nervous system more than I needed to. At least the entryway was lighted.

Just as I turned to descend the steps, the entire stairway was plunged into darkness. Someone had turned the kitchen light out! Thinking that Edith must have done it not knowing that I was on the stairs, I called to her. But there was no reply. My heart raced as terror gripped me, and I called to her again, louder. She would most certainly have heard me the second time. My voice was so loud in my ears that I'm sure I could have been heard quite clearly in the front of the house. But again there was no answer!

The teaspoon on my tray rattled against the china as I stood trembling, not knowing whether to go back to the kitchen or to continue my climb. As it turned out, I had little choice in the matter, for as I stood there, immobilized with indecision, I heard one of the steps below me creak!

"Who's there?" I called. "Is there someone there?"

I listened with all the concentration I could muster but heard only the sound of my own heart pounding in my ears. I was carrying the heavy metal serving tray and my hands weren't free, so I put my shoulder against the wall for guidance and climbed several more steps until I ran into the wall at the bend of the stairway. I was feeling my way along the turn with my shoulder when I heard the loud groan of the step which had frightened me moments before! It was six or eight steps below me.

"Who's there?" I called again. "I know you're there! Why don't you answer me?"

For a moment, I thought I detected a glow. But I couldn't be sure, for it seemed to last only a split second, and it was the sort of formless glow one occasionally sees when one's eyes are closed in the darkness. It was of such brief duration that I thought perhaps my eyes were playing tricks on me. "Why don't you answer me?" I said again.

From the depths of the darkness below me came a rasping, masculine voice in a whisper. "You must leave the house!" the voice said.

"Who are you?" I said.

"Leave!" the voice said again.

I screamed and threw the tea tray toward the voice, and the tray and its contents banged to the steps and clattered down the stairs as I kicked out towards the voice. But my foot touched nothing, and I turned and ran up the stairs, feeling my way as I climbed. There was faint light in the hallway above me, and I took the stairs two or three at a time. I climbed so quickly and made so much noise as I climbed, that I couldn't hear whether I was being pursued or not. But the adrenalin was flowing so strongly in my blood stream, giving me such incredible speed and strength, that no one could have kept pace behind me.

At the top of the stairway, I looked back over my shoulder, but the small yellow bulbs of the hallway were so widely scattered and faint that their light didn't penetrate the dark stairwell. I didn't wait to see if I was being followed but ran directly to my room. The door, which I had left open when I went downstairs, was closed. I threw it open and discovered that someone had turned all the lights off!

I left the door open and, guided by the firelight, I switched on the desk lamp and slammed the door closed. Reaching for the bolt lock, my hand came into contact with rough wood and three small holes from which screws had been withdrawn.

The lock had been removed again!

Chapter Ten

For once my wits stayed with me. I grabbed the desk chair to use as a prop under the doorknob, but it was a low-back chair and too short for use. Leaning against the door, I looked about the room in desperation for something to use as a barricade. The writing table was too small and light, and the only other piece of furniture in the room that I could move and which would offer the slightest resistance to an intruder was the heavy, overstuffed chair before the fireplace.

With strength drawn from desperation, I pushed the chair quickly against the door. Then I put my ear to the door and tried to hear if anyone was moving about the hallway, but the rain splattering against my window pane and the sound of thunder precluded my hearing anything else. I looked around the room again for something I could use as a weapon to defend myself and spotted the iron poker in the rack beside the fireplace. I ran to the fireplace and got the poker. It was solid and weighed perhaps three or four pounds. I felt more secure with it in my hand as I turned on every light in the room.

I kept my eye on the door as I moved around. But my pursuer didn't attempt to enter. Had he meant only to warn me? He wanted me to leave the house, and I most certainly would have accommodated him had I been given the chance! I would have crawled to Blackston on my hands and knees if I could have gotten out of the house. But I was doomed to spend another all-night vigil. I had no intention of budging from the room again until daylight, when I would leave the house for good—car or no car!

It wasn't until I had turned on all the lights and had just sat down on the sofa by the fireplace that I became aware of something in the air. It was the camphorous scent again —very strong! My heart pounded as I associated the odor with the lady in white. Either she had recently been in my room or she was in the room at that very moment with me! I had turned on all the lights and had seen no one. But a shock went through me as I looked across the room to the closet door. It was the only place I hadn't looked.

With poker in hand, I went to the closet door, held my breath and jerked the door open. There was nothing in the closet except my few clothes. I sighed with relief and started to close the door when I noticed my raincoat hanging there. The coat was dry, but the hardwood floor beneath it was damp with the water that had dripped from it.

I sat back on the sofa, bewildered. There was no doubt about it, I *had* confronted someone on the porch, and I had indeed fainted! Whoever it was must have carried me to my room and removed my coat and rainboots. And Edith knew! She had to know. She couldn't have been awake and not heard me shouting and ringing and pounding on the door. The man I met on the porch must have been the same one who had just followed me up the service stairs. But why?

The question didn't remain in my mind for examination, for at that very moment the lights in my room went out. I sat for several seconds in disbelief, staring around the room now only dimly illuminated by the fire. Finally, with my eye on the door, I threw two logs in the fireplace in an effort to increase the light. I tried to convince myself that electric failure was a common occurrence in rural areas during rainstorms, but I didn't believe it for a moment. I was sure that someone had removed the light fuse, and that he had done so for a purpose!

My eyes were beginning to smart before I realized that I had been sitting, frozen with fear, and staring unblinkingly at the cut-glass doorknob on the door leading to the hallway for five or ten minutes. My heart was pounding with great force in my chest, and I wondered how long one's heart could stand the strain of constant terror before it broke down, unable to keep pace with the demand placed upon it. I gripped the poker tightly and waited, knowing that whoever the man was, he would soon be coming for me. I would fight back with the poker, I thought, but then I wondered if one could hit a ghost—if it was a ghost. And I wondered if a ghost could carry a person, as I had apparently been carried from the porch to my room. Would I be swinging my weapon at the air? Was it hopeless to fight back?

I watched the doorknob and my mind wandered, searching for the tranquility of happier times and remembering pleasant moments that I thought I had long forgotten. Perhaps this is what people mean when they say their lives flash before them when experiencing a close call with death. Perhaps, like mine, their conscious minds had simply refused to accept the terrorizing present as real.

My conscious mind hadn't deserted me entirely. It immediately registered the flash of the firelight reflected by the prism of cut glass in the doorknob as the knob turned! I jumped to my feet. If I had truly entertained the idea of fighting my intruder, the thought gave way to instinct. Before I realized what I was doing, I was running into the closet and moving to the far wall in an effort to hide. It wasn't until I had reached the back wall of the closet and had turned around to face the doorway that it occurred to me that I had trapped myself in such a small area, boxed myself in where I could hardly swing the poker if it became necessary. I thought I had made the most stupid move of my life until, cringing like a child against the back wall, I felt the wall move!

I felt behind me as I watched the doorway and the fireplace across from the closet, expecting the intruder to appear in silhouette against the fireplace at any moment. The back wall was a wooden panel and was apparently mounted on a central pivot, for it swung open a foot or so when I pushed against it. I reached back beyond the panel and felt the cold dampness of a narrow passageway. It was only about two feet wide. I stuck my foot into the passageway and felt solid footing. Without looking back, I slipped into the darkness of the passageway, relieved to have found an escape route regardless of the danger.

I let the panel swing closed and made my way along the passageway as quickly as I could move in the pitch darkness, feeling the floor ahead of me with my outstretched foot and groping the damp walls with my hands. I had gone only a few feet when I reached a dead end. The passageway apparently ended at the east wall of the house. I turned around and went back towards the panel. I was passing it, my fingertips brushing along its smooth surface as I felt my way, when suddenly the panel began opening towards me!

I threw my weight against it in an effort to hold it shut, but my pursuer was stronger than I, and I was pushed back and almost pinned to the wall. I stepped aside and thought about waiting for the person to step into the passageway with me and then striking out with the poker, but I was too afraid. Instead, I turned and made my way as quickly as I could along the passageway.

The going was slow. I cringed each time my hands touched one of the countless sticky spider webs along the walls. I kept feeling a crawling sensation on my hands each time, and not knowing in the pitch darkness whether the sensation was caused by the webs clinging to my hands or by the spiders themselves, I shook my hands and brushed them against my clothing and fought to keep from crying out in my disgust and horror at the possibility that spiders were crawling on me in the blackness of the passageway.

I had gone only a short distance when, glancing back over my shoulder, I saw light. I froze for a moment, realizing that someone was now in the passageway with me, pursuing me. The flashlight beam was searching the dead end of the passageway, and I saw my pursuer clearly in silhouette against it. I could tell only that it was a man. I saw the silhouette only fleetingly, for he turned and shined the light in my direction. Fortunately the beam was weak, too weak to penetrate the distance between us.

I knew that ghosts didn't carry flashlights, so I wasn't facing the specter of Angus Harmer again. For a moment I thought my pursuer might be Harold, but I discarded the thought. Harold surely would have called out to me; this man didn't. It had to be the same man who had reached for my throat on the porch and who had warned me to leave the house when I was on the service stairs.

There was no time for cautious groping now. The man was moving slowly in my direction, and it would be only a matter of seconds before I was within range of his flashlight beam. I turned and began running along the passage, extending the poker before me to prevent my running into any more dead ends. I ran on my toes, as silently as I could, and was putting good distance between me and my pursuer when suddenly the floor gave way before me and I plunged head first, plummeting through space!

I dropped the poker and threw my hands out to keep from landing on my face. In the split second that I was in midair, I heard the poker clatter to the wooden planking below me and I realized, like a bat sending out radar signals, that my fall would be a short one. The realization came to me at the instant I crashed to the floor with a tremendous thud that must have shaken the walls of the passageway. I landed on my hands and knees, but though the fall was a short one it was no less painful.

For a moment I sat on the floor rubbing my knee and trying to get my bearings. I felt around the floor for the poker I had dropped, but found instead one of the steps I had missed in the flight of stairs I had just fallen down. I was still searching unsuccessfully for the poker when a beam of light shone above my head. From the angle of the beam, I could tell that my pursuer wasn't far behind me, but hadn't yet reached the stairway from which I had fallen. No doubt he had heard me fall, but I was below his eye level, and he hadn't yet seen me.

I scrambled to my hands and knees, away from the flight of steps, and found still another flight descending. I was apparently on a landing between stairs. I sat down on the top step and began scooting down the stairs when my left hand touched what felt like another flight of stairs leading in another direction. I felt with both hands and discovered a flight of stairs leading up to the second-story west wing.

Without hesitation, I began crawling up the stairs on my hands and feet. I did so quickly, for it was easier for me to move with my hands before me. Below, the light grew stronger as the man who was following me came closer to the staircase. If I could reach the top before he reached the landing upon which I had fallen, he wouldn't have a chance of spotting me, for the stairs I was climbing were to the left of the passageway.

There was an abrupt turn at the top of the staircase to a passageway which ran the full length of the west-wing bedrooms. Once I had scrambled around the turn to the passageway so that I could no longer be seen from below, I stopped and looked back. For the first time since I had entered the passageway, there was hope of my eluding the man who was pursuing me. Not only could I not be seen from the landing below, but I had full command of the stairway as well. If my pursuer followed me up the narrow staircase I had just taken, I could take him by surprise, pushing him off the narrow steps. I shuddered at the thought of having to do it, but I was frightened out of my wits, and I knew that if I didn't stop him, I might sooner or later run into another dead end and would be easy prey for him, trapped like a senseless animal in a maze.

I watched the light below as it scanned every inch of the passageway and grew more intense as the shadowy figure of the man finally came into view, descending the staircase from which I had fallen. He stopped at the landing and probed the darkness of the other descending stairwell with his flashlight before directing the beam to the landing and finding the poker I had dropped. He picked up the poker, then searched the staircase I had just ascended. I watched the splotch of light move towards me and stepped back around the corner as it flashed past me, striking the wall before me where the staircase turned. The light hung there, fixed on the wall, and I held my breath, thinking that he would begin climbing the stairs at any moment, and dreading what I would have to do if he did.

But the beam vanished from the wall, and I peeked around the corner again, hoping that he hadn't directed the beam of light to his feet so that he could see to climb the stairs. He stood motionless, shining the light into the darkness of the descending stairwell once more. In the periphery of the flashlight beam, I could see that he was carrying the poker. My heart jumped when it dawned on me that the instrument I had chosen for my self-defense might now be used against me!

Not only hope, but luck, too, was with me, for the man finally committed himself, continuing down the stairwell out of sight. Breathing a sigh of relief, I slumped to the floor, unable to move. I breathed deeply in an effort to relax and to slow my pounding heart. My lungs ached from the frightened, shallow breaths I had been taking, and though I was crouched down to gather my strength, my legs still trembled from weakness and my right knee hurt from the fall I had taken. I rubbed my knee, fought back tears of anguish, and tried to gather my thoughts and courage.

The person hunting me in the lower passageway would soon undoubtedly discover that I had not taken the lower stairwell, and would double back. With him searching for me, I had to get out of the passage as fast as I could. I knew that he would expect me to return to my room, so I couldn't do that. My only recourse was to press on, searching for a way out of the passageway as I went.

Wanting a few more moments' rest, I looked into the darkness below, watching for light. But a horrendous thought occurred to me, sending me scrambling to my feet again. My pursuer probably knew the passageways very well. What would prevent him from turning his flashlight off and pursuing me in the darkness? For all I knew, he could have been slipping quietly up the stairway towards me at that very moment!

I held my breath, listening for evidence of movement on the steps below me. When I was sure that there was no sound, I began groping my way along the west passageway towards the front of the house. I moved along, feeling the walls to each side of me, and soon felt the unmistakable smoothness of wood paneling. I gathered, judging from the short distance I had traveled, that I was outside the back west-wing bedroom, the bedroom facing mine and separated from it by the second-floor library. I put my ear to the panel and listened for a moment. But I could hear nothing, and, indeed, had expected to hear nothing because the west-wing bedrooms were unoccupied.

Pulling the panel open, I was surprised to see light beneath the closed closet door and to see that the closet was filled with clothes! I wondered why a closet full of clothes would be kept in an unused bedroom but decided that they were probably old clothes that the family hadn't bothered to discard.

I slipped into the closet and let the panel swing shut behind me. In contrast to the pitch blackness of the passageway, the closet seemed well lighted, even bright, from the faint light source. I waited for a moment, looking around the closet and letting my eyes become accustomed to light again. The heavy scent of mothballs was suffocating, strongly camphorous. *Camphorous,* I thought. And a chill went through me when I remembered that it was this same camphorous odor I had smelled when first seeing the lady in white! Had it been mothballs I had smelled? Was her bridal gown permeated with the scent?

It was an appalling thought. But even more appalling was the thought that the back west-wing bedroom whose closet I now occupied might have been Julia's room! Or, worse yet, it might *still* be her room! Could it be, I thought, that she was still alive—perhaps mad—and being kept prisoner here?

My hands became moist with the thought, and I began to tremble again. I had to get a grip on myself, I thought. I had to exercise some restraint on my rampant imagination. Surely, I reasoned, no one could have been kept prisoner in the room. After all, the panel wasn't sealed shut, and both Harold and Edith *had* to know about the secret passageways. Still the nagging thoughts persisted. Perhaps they didn't consider Julia violent. Perhaps a false report of Julia's death had been made to hide the fact that there was madness in the Harmer family. In those days there was a stigma attached to insanity. Could it be that Edith became upset with my stories about Julia's attacking me simply because she refused to believe that Julia was capable of violence? And if Edith didn't want anyone—especially Mark—to know that Julia was alive, she might well invent

99

the story of Julia's ghost to cover the possibility that I might run into Julia by accident during my stay at Harmer House. That made sense. It didn't explain my seeing Angus Harmer, or the man who was chasing me through the passageways, but it offered a reasonable explanation for many of the questions that had plagued me since my arrival at Harmer House.

I placed my ear to the closet door and listened for a full minute or two. There were no sounds at all from the bedroom. If I could get through the room to the hall, I could face Edith with my theory, and convince her that there was no need to put me through this torture. She could have the house, and the secret of Julia would stay with me so far as I was concerned.

I turned the doorknob as silently as I could, holding my breath and praying that the room would be empty. Opening the door a crack, I peered out. I could see the bed, which was made, unslept in and covered with an old-fashioned patchwork quilt, a few occasional chairs and a small round table in the corner. I saw no one. The hinges on the door squeaked loudly as I opened the door further. I stepped back, ready to bolt for the passageway panel, but moments passed and there was still no sound in the room. Cautiously I stuck my head out of the closet and glanced quickly around the room. To my relief, it was empty, and I slipped through the opening in an effort to keep the door from squeaking again, and entered the room.

The light came from a small lamp on the writing table across from the closet door. And I gasped when I saw the silver-framed black and white photograph next to the lamp. It was a picture of the lady in white!

Moving across the room on tiptoe, I took a closer look at the photograph. It was apparently of Julia, taken when she was eighteen or twenty. She was dressed in her white bridal gown, the veil pulled back over her head, her long blonde hair falling casually about her shoulders. She was an attractive girl with a trim figure, large dark eyes, high cheek bones, full lips in a pleasant smile, and a beautifully clear complexion. She was the image of the lady in white I had seen in the hallway—except, of course, for her face, which I couldn't see behind the heavy veil.

The photograph mesmerized me and it gave me the chills. As I looked at it, I remembered her mad laughter and the terrifying scene of her standing above me, the knife raised high above her head. I was still examining the photograph when I had a strange premonition that someone was going to enter the room! At that moment, the bedroom door swung slowly open and there, knife in hand, stood the real lady in white!

Chapter Eleven

Her bridal gown was extremely yellowed with age and quite wrinkled, but it was the same one I had been studying in the photograph. I could see closely now the tear in the bodice with the dark red stain around and below the tear, and Edith's words echoed in my mind as I stood staring at the spot: *She killed herself with a knife! Held the point to her heart and fell on it! Does that please you, Miss Gilmore?*

My God! I thought. I wanted to back away from her, but I couldn't move. I was transfixed by the specter! I wanted to run; I wanted to lunge at her—pushing her out of my way—so that I could escape down the hall. I wanted to do something—*anything!* But I couldn't move!

She remained standing in the doorway, her hands hanging loosely at her sides, the knife clutched in her right hand. And that chilling laugh erupted from behind her heavy veil. "You shouldn't have come back," she said.

I was shocked to hear her speak. And she spoke in such a low whisper, an almost pathetic, regretful whisper, that I wasn't at all sure that she had spoken or, if she had, that I had heard her correctly. It was as though the sound of her voice was coming from far away.

"I . . . I'm leaving," I stammered. "I'm leaving in the morning. My car. . . ."

"It's too late," she said. "Too late, too late," she repeated.

"No!" I said. "I tried to leave earlier, but my car wouldn't start. I'm going down to see Miss Harmer now, and I'll leave in the morning. I don't want the house!"

She shook her head negatively and took a step in my direction. "Too late," she said again.

I stepped back two or three paces. She took another step, raising her knife.

"Get away from me!" I screamed. "Let me out of here!"

"Don't you see it's too late?" she said.

"It's *not* too late!" I insisted.

She continued to shake her head, moving slowly forward, stalking me. I backed up, but I realized that her moves were well calculated. She wasn't going to lunge at me. There would be no chance to outflank her, to run around her and into the hall. She was moving slowly and with deliberation, cornering me!

"Get away from me!" I said.

She laughed again—if one could call that animal-like sound a laugh. I looked around for something I could defend myself with, but there was nothing within reach. I feigned a move to my left, towards the writing table, then bolted for the closet as fast as I could run, fully expecting to have a knife plunged between my shoulder blades at any moment. But, as before, the adrenalin had been flowing through my system, thanks to my constant state of fear, and my speed was astounding even to me as I slammed my shoulder against the panel and plunged into the dark passageway, banging the panel closed behind me.

Her mad laughter was still ringing in my ears as I stumbled blindly along the passageway without caution until I ran into what I thought to be another dead end and realized that in my panic I had lost all sense of direction. I groped around the walls and found that the passageway took a sharp turn to the left. I vaguely remembered having made another turn moments earlier. I no longer had the faintest idea where I was. I was lost!

I must have wandered in the black labyrinth for perhaps fifteen minutes, pausing every few steps to listen for the footfalls of the lady in white, who I was sure must have followed me from her room. I had eluded her, but I was sure that she knew the passageways well and could easily make up for the initial lead I had gotten on her. Being in the strange dark passageway was bad enough when I had maintained my sense of direction. Before, at least, I could have found my way back to my room if necessary. But now I had taken several more dizzying turns which further added to my disorientation, and I had found no way out of the dreadful maze.

Finally, I did find another staircase which seemed to lead to the first floor. The steps were so narrow that I had to slip sideways down them, holding on to the rough wall boards to keep from falling as I descended. Reaching the first-floor level, I moved straight ahead, heartened by the hope of at last finding my way out. But my hopes came to an abrupt end—literally—when I came to still another dead end.

I came very close to hysteria. I wanted to run screaming through the passageways and pounding on the walls. Fortunately, though, my judgment was not that affected, and I knew that if I were ever going to find my way out, I had to remain calm and clear-headed. I knew also that both the man who had followed me and the lady in white would eventually overtake me if I didn't keep moving. And the last thing I wanted was to be trapped at one of the passageway's dead ends.

In order to keep from panicking, I thought only of my immediate problem: to find a panel leading out of the passageways. In the back of my mind, though, I knew that neither of my alternatives was any good. If I remained where I was, I would inevitably be found by one of my pursuers. By moving on, I ran the distinct risk of overrunning one of *them!* But at least the latter alternative offered me a chance to discover a way out before someone discovered me.

I retraced my steps to the stairway and continued on. Despite the dampness, I was choked from the age-old layers of dust I was dislodging from the walls with my hands as I groped my way in the darkness. And I was beginning to wonder if I was doomed to wander forever in the seemingly endless maze of passages when I was brought up short by voices! I stopped and strained to listen. They were the voices of a man and a woman. I could hear them only faintly, and they were moving neither towards me nor away from me, for their volume remained unchanged. They were somewhere ahead of me. I moved forward as silently as I could, gripped with the fear that they might be the voices of the man and the woman in white! As I came to a turn in the passageway, the voices seemed louder, and at the turn I saw a pinpoint shaft of light!

Realizing that the voices were not coming from the passageway, but from one of the rooms, I moved quickly towards the light and discovered that it was coming from a small hole in a wooden panel. Nearing it, I recognized the voices as those of Edith and Harold! I peeked through the hole to find that I was looking into the downstairs library through one of the bookcases.

I could see Edith, who was sitting in her wheel chair across from the fireplace, but I couldn't see Harold. From the tone of his voice, I knew that he was angry. And from the way Edith's eyes were moving back and forth, I assumed that she was watching Harold pace back and forth before the fireplace. I pushed on the panel to gain entrance to the library, but it wouldn't open. I was about to call to them for help when I heard Harold mention my name.

"But I don't think it's right any longer," he said. "Miss Gilmore took a nasty fall in the passageway, and she could be seriously hurt! God knows where she is now, if she hasn't fallen down another of the staircases and broken her neck!"

"I don't have to justify my plan to you!" Edith snapped. "And, frankly, I'm very disappointed that you even *question* my orders. I had expected you to be loyal, Harold, after all these years."

"We're not talking about loyalty, Miss Harmer. After thirty years' service to Mr. Harmer, I doubt that you can question my loyalty, and I'm offended that you're trying to do so! There's just no sense to this business with Miss Gilmore anymore!"

"Oh, indeed?" Edith said. "Keeping Harmer House in the Harmer family doesn't make sense to you? Doesn't involve loyalty?"

"She seems like a nice young woman. I'm sure she'd let us stay if she knew that you wanted to. She didn't ask for the—"

"I should beg a stranger to let me stay in my own house?" Edith interrupted. "Are you serious?"

"It's Miss Gilmore's house now—according to Mr. Harmer's wishes."

"It's *my* house!" Edith shouted. "And no piece of paper is going to take it away from me! She's not a Harmer!"

"Something could be arranged without this dangerous trickery."

"I know what I'm doing," Edith said.

"I wonder."

"What do you mean by *that?*"

"I mean that I'm beginning to think that you have something personal against Miss Gilmore," Harold said. "I went along with you in trying to scare her away—even though I questioned your methods and failed to see how your plan could accomplish anything. I did it out of loyalty, Miss Harmer, but I can't stand by and see her injured. It appears to me that you're not simply trying to scare her off."

"Really?" Edith retorted. "Then what do you think I'm trying to do?"

"I don't know. But it seems to me that you're taking a rather sadistic pleasure in torturing her!"

"Nonsense!"

"Then why are you still having me disable her car? She's frightened out of her wits now; she'd leave this moment if we'd let her. That's what you want, isn't it? Or is it?"

"Of course it's what I want. But not just yet."

"Not just yet!" Harold repeated. "It's a wonder the girl hasn't been driven out of her mind. It's inhuman! It's bad enough having the lady in white haunting the grounds since Julia's death! I've had a mind to quit because of her several times myself. Her presence alone should be enough to frighten Miss Gilmore away. She's apparently seen her."

"Yes, apparently," Edith said.

"And as though that weren't enough, you've got her believing that she saw Mr. Harmer's ghost as well!"

"What she *imagines,* is not my responsibility."

"I think we're both responsible," Harold said. "And I won't be a party to this any longer."

"You'll do exactly as I say if you want to continue working for *me!*"

"No, Miss Harmer, I'm sorry."

"Then you don't want to remain at Harmer House?"

"Of course I'd like to remain, but frightening Miss Gilmore from the house is one thing. Holding her prisoner and subjecting her to this mental cruelty is criminal! You've asked too much of me already. I nearly scared her to death on the porch this evening, and her fall in the passageway could have done her permanent injury."

"Perhaps you've changed alliances. Is that what you're up to?"

Harold came into view, passing Edith on his way to the door, then turning to face her. "What do you mean by that?" he asked.

"That you might be thinking of going to work for Miss Gilmore—here at Harmer House, maybe?"

"I doubt that she'd want any part of me after she learns what we've been doing to her," Harold said.

"She'll never know."

"Oh, but she will. I'm going to find her right now and see her safely into town."

"No!" Edith said. "You'll do nothing of the sort! Find her and see her safely to her room, if you wish, but she's not to leave and she's to know nothing!"

Harold shook his head gravely. "I'll not have her bodily harm or mental breakdown on my conscience," he said. Then, angered, he added, "For her own sanity, I'm going to tell her about this vicious game we've been playing."

"You're a fool!" Edith said. "She could bring charges against us!"

"I was a fool to go along with your scheme in the first place. You're asking too much of my loyalty. You're doing dastardly things in the name of the Harmer family. Mr. Harmer would have hated us for what we've done. You've gone too far already."

Harold turned and walked quickly from the library. Edith followed him quickly in her wheel chair. "Harold!" she said. "Harold! I forbid this!"

If Harold replied, I couldn't hear him. I remained staring into the library long after they had left the room. I was stunned! So it was Harold who had assailed me on the porch and who had chased me through the passageways! And for what? For Harmer House? I would gladly give it to Edith.

Knowing that they could give me directions out of the passageways, I shouted to them and pounded on the wall. But they had apparently gone to another part of the house, for my shouts went unanswered.

So it had been Edith's plan to discredit me all along, I thought. This alone made me feel immeasurably better. And knowing Harold's role—knowing that the strange man wasn't pursuing me—helped to assuage my fear. But still there was the lady in white. I had been wrong in my guess that she was alive and insane and being kept secretly at Harmer House. From what Harold had said, she was indeed a ghost—one that Harold himself feared. Was she hostile towards me because she was doomed forever to haunt Harmer House and wanted her mother to remain there? Was that possible? And what of Angus Harmer? Both Harold and Edith had denied the existence of his ghost. But no matter, I thought. I would soon be rid of the cursed place.

I felt sure that there had to be another panel or two along the way, opening into the dining room or Harold's room, so I continued along the passageway, searching the walls for the smooth surface of paneling. I made my search slowly and methodically. My extreme tension had left me until I remembered that the ghost of the lady in white was real and that I had made a terrible racket when pounding on the wall and shouting—drawing attention to my position in the passageway.

Fear gripped me once more. My search for the paneling in the walls became more frenzied, for I knew that somewhere in those dark passages the hostile ghost, armed with a knife, was stalking me!

Chapter Twelve

If there were passageway panels to the dining room or to Harold's room, I couldn't find them. For several minutes, I searched the walls which bordered the rooms. But it was useless. So near and yet so far, I thought. Only a thin wall now lay between my escape from Harmer House with Harold's help, and danger for my very life in that Godforsaken dark passageway. I had never been so frustrated in my life!

I knew that Harold must have been searching the labyrinth of secret passages for me at that very moment. And it was only natural for me to want to call out to him. But I didn't dare. My calls to Edith and Harold had done damage enough, I was sure. For all I knew, the lady in white was moving towards that spot outside the library at that very moment. I knew, too, that I couldn't remain in the west wing if I wanted to leave Harmer House with my life!

Just past what I judged to be Harold's room, the passageway turned to the right, running along the back of the house. I crept cautiously, pausing every few feet to listen, but all was unearthly blackness and silence. I kept watching for the beam of Harold's flashlight ahead of me as I made my way, inch by inch, my hands groping the walls on either side of me. Then, pausing to reach arm's length before me to be sure that the way was clear, I'd take another two steps before sweeping my arms before me again. Each time I reached out, I did so in dread that my fingertips would touch the knife-wielding specter that could be waiting for me at any point along the way.

When I reached what I thought to be the halfway point in the passage which bordered the back of the house, the wall seemed to give way to the right. Probing into the darkness with my outstretched hands, I found a stairway which rose above me. Since I had had no luck in finding a way out of the first-floor passage, and since I didn't know what lay before me along the route I was taking, I climbed the staircase, knowing that at least it would eventually lead to the passage I had taken from my room.

The steps ascended to a landing before continuing to the second floor. On the landing I was overjoyed to find the smooth wood of a narrow panel. I pushed on the panel, but it was solid. My heart sank at the thought of finding another panel that had been apparently sealed. In my desperation, I felt along the entire width and length of the panel and discovered hinges. Grabbing the unhinged side, I pulled, and the heavy panel swung towards me with a loud, rasping groan.

It opened to a gloomy area which was almost dark. To my right, though, I saw faint light coming from above, and I realized that the panel had opened onto the landing of the service stairs where I had hurled the tea tray earlier in the evening.

The stairway below was dark, for the kitchen light was still out. I let the panel swing shut behind me and descended the stairs to the kitchen, holding tightly to the rail and treading lightly for fear that the tea tray and its contents would still be scattered about the stairs. There was light coming from the hallway at the far end of the kitchen and, as I approached, I could see that the light was coming from the direction of Harold's room just down the hall.

Fear and tension left me as I stepped into the hall and saw a shadow fall across the threshold of Harold's room, where he had apparently passed between the light and the doorway. But I stopped in utter horror as the shadow lengthened from Harold's room across the hallway floor. It was the unmistakable outline of the lady in white!

Electrified, I stepped back into the kitchen and backed into the dark corner by the cupboard only feet from the doorway. My chest contracted as though in a vise, and my heart pounded so loudly in my ears that I thought for sure the lady in white had heard it. The shadow fell across the floor in front of me, and I held my breath to keep from crying out when I realized that she was coming towards the kitchen!

Her appearance in the doorway was worse than any nightmarish vision I had ever experienced. She was so close to me that I could have reached out and touched her! She paused in the doorway for a moment. She had only to glance to her right to see me. A dozen terrifying thoughts occurred to me as she stood there. I wondered if she could sense my presence. I wondered if she had heard the rusty groan of the panel on the landing. I wondered if she was simply waiting for me to make a move.

She stood motionless, as though listening. Her hands were resting at her sides. And in her right hand was the ever-present knife, its blade glistening in the light from

Harold's room. I had held my breath from the moment she appeared and I wanted desperately to breathe. But she was so terribly close that I was afraid to.

I nearly jumped when at last she moved. But she looked neither right nor left, and walked slowly with an almost trancelike gliding movement that made my skin crawl. She passed me, her hands still hanging limply at her sides, and walked the full length of the kitchen before stopping again at the foot of the service stairs. I cringed in my dark corner, not moving a muscle. It was the most crucial moment of my life! I took a breath, praying that she wouldn't hear me, but my lungs were aching for air, and I was afraid that I'd pass out from lack of oxygen if I didn't breathe.

She remained motionless, peering up into the darkness of the stairwell. She had only to turn around to see me! And from the way she seemed to be deliberating about climbing the stairs, I was sure that she was going to turn around. For a fleeting moment, I considered darting through the doorway and into the hall. And I almost did so. But miraculously, despite my terror of the moment, my brain was functioning, and I realized that even though her back was turned, by stepping into the doorway, my shadow would have been cast across the kitchen by the light from Harold's room, and she would have discovered me.

But finally she stirred, and my heart leaped. I was ready to take flight if she turned. I would break for the front door and run into the countryside. But she moved forward, slowly climbing the steps until she rose from sight, enveloped by the darkness.

Even after I could no longer see her, I waited for a full minute or two, listening for the hinges in the panel at the landing. There was no sound, though. And I knew that she must have continued up the stairs to the second floor and my room.

With my eyes fixed on the stairs, I slipped through the

kitchen doorway and into the hall. My foot skidded from under me and I nearly fell, and I again held my breath. Had I fallen, she most certainly would have heard me. Without thinking, I looked to see what had made me lose my footing. The floor was smeared with something wet beneath my foot. I realized that this was where the lady in white had stood in the doorway. Inches away there was another spot on the floor. I became nauseous when it dawned on me that the spots were crimson red—like blood!

I ran into Harold's room and was immediately stunned by the impact of the sight before me! I had to clamp my hands over my mouth to keep from screaming, and I doubled over, lowering my head to force blood into it in an effort to maintain consciousness. Harold lay sprawled on the floor before me, face down, his left arm pinned beneath his body, his right arm outstretched, a flashlight still gripped tightly in his hand. The back of his black suitcoat was shredded in several places, and the blood-soaked shreds of his once-white shirt protruded from the slashes. His face was turned towards his desk and his lifeless blue eyes were open and unseeing. Beyond question, he was dead!

My legs threatened to buckle beneath me, and I grabbed on to a table for support, shaking my head violently to clear it. If I fainted, I would be the lady in white's second victim—and her easiest prey! Somehow I managed to remain on my feet. And after fighting myself to break the hypnotic horror with which I was staring at Harold's lifeless body, I backed into the hallway, sick to my stomach and gasping for air.

The lady in white had gone up the stairs only moments before. I had no time to lose. I had to shake the sickness that was overcoming me. I had to bolt for the front door and run, putting Harmer House as far behind me as possible. But now there was a murder! I tried to recall if there was a farmhouse between Harmer House and Blackston, but I couldn't concentrate. I wanted only to escape the place and call the police or find shelter until morning.

But I remembered Edith!

In her wheel chair, Edith would be helpless. And even if it was the ghost of her daughter, she wouldn't be safe—no one would be safe, for Julia was quite obviously mad! I couldn't leave Edith alone and defenseless. I knew that I'd have to go to her room, find something to defend us with, and stay with her until the cook arrived in the morning.

I ran down the hall past the darkened living room and across the marble floor of the entrance way, scanning the front staircases and the second-story landing as I ran, afraid that the lady in white would be standing there, staring down at me as she had done before. But she was nowhere in sight.

Edith's door was unlocked, and I burst into her room without knocking. The room was alight, but empty. Her bed was still made. I ran from her room, again scanning the staircases and the landing above. There was no sign of movement, no sound. I stopped in the center of the entrance way, not knowing which way to turn. The library and dining room were dark. I knew that she wasn't in Harold's room or the kitchen, and the living room too had been dark when I passed it.

I went to the library door. Edith was usually in the library, and I thought she might have returned to it after talking to Harold. Perhaps she had sat before the fireplace in the dark and had fallen asleep. I stopped at the doorway, however, suddenly seized with the horrifying thought that the lady in white could have come downstairs and entered one of the dark rooms while I was in Harold's room. There had been plenty of time for her to do so. I was afraid, too, that I might find Edith dead in her wheel chair!

I looked into the library. I could see very little. The fire

114

in the fireplace was low and gave but little light. I edged into the room, ready to bolt at the slightest provocation. I looked for the whiteness of the gown in the darkness but could see nothing. There seemed to be no movement, so I edged still further until I reached a small table with a lamp on it to the left of the door. Switching the lamp on, I looked quickly around the room. There was no one there, but on the floor, directly before the bookcase through which I had overheard Harold and Edith's conversation, lay Edith's overturned wheel chair—empty!

Thinking that the lady in white must have dragged her into the passageway, I pushed and pulled on the bookcase that had at one time been a passageway panel. But it was definitely sealed shut. Hoping that Edith might still be alive, I called to her. But there was no answer. Frustrated and emboldened by my concern for her welfare and her helpless state, I picked up a poker from the fireplace and ran from the library into the high-domed entrance hall. "Edith!" I screamed. "Edith?"

"Julia?"

It was Edith's voice, from far off, and I couldn't tell from which direction it was coming.

"Edith, it's me, Elizabeth. Where are you?"

"Julia?" Edith uttered again, faintly.

She was calling Julia! The acoustics were so bad in the entrance hall that her voice sounded as though it were coming from several directions. Had Julia dragged her to the second floor? I looked into the shadows along the banister which bordered the domed hallway but I could see no one. *"Where are you?"* I screamed.

"I'm here, Julia," Edith said calmly.

Why was she calling to Julia? "Where?" I screamed again. "I can't see you!"

"In the living room, dear," she called.

I ran to the living room and looked in. It was very dark. "Edith?" I called.

There was no answer.

"Edith?" I repeated. "Why don't you answer me?"

There was complete silence. I started to take a step into the room, poker ready, when suddenly, out of the shadows of the living room, stepped the lady in white!

I screamed and backed into the hallway. "What have you done to Edith!?" I cried.

The lady in white said nothing, but moved through the doorway into the hall towards me, her knife raised above her head, and I could see the blood on her knife! I backed against the hallway wall, realizing that I was too late to save Edith. She must have used Edith to lure me into the living room, then killed her before I entered!

"Get back!" I screamed, jabbing the poker at her. "Get away from me!"

But she continued moving towards me, the knife raised high above her head, the bubbling, hideous laughter erupting from deep within her. I grabbed the poker with both hands to swing it at her with all my strength, and as I did so, I wondered if one could hit a ghost, wondered if the poker would pass through her body as though I were trying to hit a vaporous mist! And at that very moment, as she came within my range, she was stopped, seemingly startled by the most beautiful sound I've ever heard.

The doorbell rang!

I couldn't believe my ears. I ran down the hall towards the entrance, looking back over my shoulder as I ran. As the doorbell rang the second time, the lady in white backed into the living room, and I ran headlong into the front door.

Before I could even open the door I heard his voice: "Elizabeth? It's me, Mark!"

Chapter Thirteen

I jerked the door open and virtually plunged into Mark's arms, almost bowling him over from the impact. The sight of him released my pent-up emotions in a flood of tears, and I sobbed uncontrollably, clinging to him with all my strength. He put his arms around me and stroked my hair, trying to console me in his bewilderment.

"What's wrong?" he said. "What on earth are you doing with that poker in your hand?"

It's a wonder that he didn't think I'd cracked completely, the way I had jerked the door open, crying with hysteria and leaping at him with a poker in my hand! I had forgotten I was carrying the dreadful thing. I dropped it, and it clattered to the porch. My arm and wrist and hand were numb from gripping it so tightly.

"He's dead!" I sobbed. "And she may have killed Edith, too!"

Mark pushed me back so that he could see my face. "Control yourself, Elizabeth!" he said. "You're not making any sense! Who's dead? What are you talking about?"

"Harold! He's been stabbed to death by the lady in white—by Julia!"

Mark looked at me in disbelief. "Harold's *dead?*" he repeated. "Are you serious?"

"Yes," I sobbed. "And she has Edith now . . . dragged

her out of her wheel chair. They're in the living room, but I couldn't get to her to help!"

"No!" Mark said, shaking his head. "Surely. . . ."

"Yes!" I screamed. "Yes. There's no time for explanations! They're in the living room. I'm afraid she might have killed Edith too!"

Though I was exhorting him to action, in my hysteria I was still gripping him so tightly that he could hardly move. He pulled my arms from about him and ran towards the living room. I followed close behind him. "Be careful!" I warned him. "She has a knife!"

He pushed me behind him and led the way into the living room. It took several seconds for our eyes to become accustomed to the darkness. We could see no one. "Edith?" Mark called. There was no answer, no movement. Mark went into the room, found a lamp and turned it on.

The room was empty, but a passageway panel behind a long table was ajar. Mark stepped into the passageway and again called to Edith. But again there was no answer, and he backed out of the passageway. "Do you have a flashlight?" he asked.

"There's one in Harold's room," I said, shuddering at the memory of Harold's lifeless hand clutching the flashlight.

We ran down the hall to Harold's room. Mark stopped abruptly in the doorway, staring into the room. "My God!" he said, looking down at Harold's body. "You'd better wait here in the hall."

"No!" I said, following him into the room. I didn't want to look at Harold's body again, but I had no intention of leaving Mark's side so long as we remained in the house.

Mark examined Harold's body, feeling for a pulse. I avoided looking at Harold again, focusing my attention instead on the doorway, fully expecting the lady in white to enter, knife in hand, at any moment.

"He's dead, all right," Mark said, prying the flashlight from Harold's stiff, tight grasp. "He's been stabbed half a dozen times! Only a *maniac* could have done this!"

"It was Julia," I said, not turning around.

Mark got to his feet and approached me, eyeing me levelly. "Elizabeth," he said. "Julia's been dead for more than twenty years!"

"I know. Don't you think I know *that?* But Harold said she's been haunting the grounds ever since her death. I overheard him talking to Edith about her. He was afraid of her, and he said he'd have left the place long ago if it hadn't been for his loyalty to Angus."

Mark stared at me for a moment, searchingly, then shook his head as though he simply couldn't comprehend what I was telling him.

"It's true!" I assured him. "I saw her. She attacked me!"

"Are you sure she's got Edith?"

"Positive," I said, breaking into tears again. "I found Edith's wheel chair overturned in the library. And when I called to her, afraid for her safety, she answered me from the living room. She kept calling to Julia! She must have been trying to warn me that Julia was in the room with her. But I didn't understand at the time.

"When I tried to get to her, Julia blocked the doorway and threatened me with her bloody knife—just as you rang the doorbell. It was horrible!"

"How do you know it was Julia?"

"Because of what Harold said about her and because I saw her picture in her bedroom upstairs. She wears the same wedding gown she wore in the photograph."

"I'll have to search the passageways for her," Mark said. "You'd better take my car and get the sheriff. I'll see you out to the car."

"No. I want to stay with you."

"You'd be much safer out of here."

"No," I insisted. "Maybe I could help you. I don't want

you searching the passageways alone. Besides, I don't know these back roads at night."

"All right," Mark said, resigned. "If you insist. She can't have gotten far with Edith. She'd have to drag her, unless. . . ."

"I know. She may have killed Edith, too. She never answered my call again."

"My God!" Mark said again, looking down at Harold's body. "I can't believe this!"

We went back through the living room and into the passageway. I held tightly to Mark's jacket and we moved quickly with the aid of Harold's flashlight. We kept calling to Edith as we searched. But there was no answer. We soon decided not to call out anymore, for in doing so, we were letting Julia know exactly where we were at all times.

Without the slightest hesitation, Mark walked quickly through the passageways with obvious familiarity, searching the darkness before us and behind us as we moved.

"We'll check the tunnel that leads outside, first," he said.

"I didn't know there was one."

"Yes. There's an exit that leads to the grounds behind the house."

"You've been in the passageways before?" I asked, astonished.

"Angus showed me through the passageways many times when I was a boy," Mark said.

The panel opened to the grounds behind a large clump of oleander bushes. Mark searched the rain-drenched ground below with the flashlight. "No footprints," he said. "They have to be in the house somewhere. No one has left from here."

We retraced our steps and continued our search throughout the passages, going through each of the panels and searching the rooms as we went. But to no avail. We had searched for nearly half an hour before finally returning to the living room. Then we went through the dining room, the library, Edith's room and the game room, turning on all the lights as we searched. Still, we found nothing.

"It's hopeless to look through the passages again," Mark said. "We've searched every foot of them. They could be anywhere. They might even have followed along behind us every step of the way for all we know. We'll check the upstairs rooms which can't be reached from the passages—Mr. Harmer's room and the front west-wing bedrooms. If there's no trace of them there, then we've done all we possibly can. We'll just have to go into town and get the sheriff."

We left the dining room and went down the hall and through the kitchen to the service stairs.

"There won't be any light in Mr. Harmer's room," I said. "Someone pulled the fuse to the east wing, I think."

"The flashlight will do," Mark said, climbing the stairs ahead of me.

The service steps creaked loudly beneath our feet as we climbed them. I was just a step or two behind Mark and was on the landing as he began climbing the second flight, when I was terror-stricken by the unmistakable rasping groan of the rusty hinges in the passageway panel that opened onto the landing. Mark continued climbing, no doubt thinking that the noise was made by one of the steps I had trod. But I was so startled by the dreadful and familiar sound that I missed the first step and fell forward, sprawling on the steps. *"Mark!"* I screamed as I fell.

Mark jerked the flashlight beam in my direction just in time to catch the white blur as the lady in white lunged at me! I rolled to my left side and, at that very instant, I heard a sickening, dull thump as she drove the point of her knife into the step where I had lain, missing me by inches! And at the same time, she threw her full weight upon me, pinning me to the stairs and wrenching the point from the wooden step to thrust it into me!

I screamed and closed my eyes in terror, pinned helplessly to the stairs and cringing from the knife-thrust that I knew was coming. But the fatal blow didn't come. I felt her weight suddenly lift from me, and I heard scuffling above me. I opened my eyes.

The flashlight was still in Mark's hand. And its beam was dancing crazily around the walls and ceiling and stairs as he struggled with the lady in white directly above me, trying to disarm her. But she was fighting with the desperation and strength of a wild animal. And in the eerie, darting light, they looked as though they were doing a grotesque ritual dance. She was spinning, thrashing, wrenching and jerking violently in an effort to escape Mark's grasp until Mark lost his footing and skidded the several steps to the landing below, dragging her with him.

As they crashed to the landing below, Mark lost his grip on the flashlight, and it clattered down the steps and went out, plunging the stairwell into darkness!

I jumped to my feet. *"Mark!"* I screamed.

"Stay there!" Mark cried. "Don't come down here!"

I tried to see into the darkness below, but it was no use. I could hear only scuffling, bodies thumping into the wall on the landing, and the occasional blood-curdling, feral sounds of Julia fighting back—vicious, wolf-like growling sounds. And then the sound that assaulted my nerves like an electric shock: first the grunting, throaty sound of Julia in violent physical exertion, then the shocking groan of Mark in pain! She had stabbed him!

"Mark!" I called.

"I'm all right!" Mark responded. "Stay there!"

The scuffling continued for a moment. I was frozen in terror, not knowing what to do. I wanted to help, but I couldn't see to help. I couldn't see anything. Suddenly the darkness was pierced by Julia's terrible scream, followed by the sickening continual thumping sound of a body falling down the flight of stairs to the kitchen. And then the quick footfalls of someone running down the steps. "Mark?" I called again.

"Wait," Mark yelled, his voice distant. "It's all right now. Stay there a moment."

I gazed into the darkness, not knowing what was happening, when suddenly the stairwell was lighted again and I realized that Mark had turned on the kitchen light.

"You can come down now, Elizabeth," Mark called.

I ran down the steps to the landing, then started down the lower flight to the kitchen but stopped, awestruck, when I saw the twisted form of the lady in white lying on her back at the foot of the stairs. I could see only the lower portion of her, for Mark was bending over her, his back to me. The position she was lying in reminded me of my father's twisted body, and I didn't want to go near her. "Are you all right?" I asked Mark.

He looked up at me over his shoulder. "Yes, I'm okay," he said. And then, apparently seeing the fear in my eyes, he added: "It's all over. You can come down now."

I edged down the stairs, watching him take her pulse. He shook his head. "I can't believe it!" he said.

"What is it?" I said. But when I reached the bottom step and could see her completely from that vantage point, I realized that there was no need for Mark to answer my question. The answer was self-evident, and I gasped in astonishment.

There, at my feet, lay Edith!

The veil and blonde wig she had worn lay nearby where they had fallen as she tumbled down the steps. The knife, with the dark blood stains, lay on the floor several feet away.

"She lost her balance and fell backward," Mark said. "I can't believe her strength!"

"Is she dead?" I asked.

"No. She's out cold, though. And I'd say, from the looks of that arm, it's probably broken. It's a wonder she didn't break her neck!"

"But I thought she was *paralyzed!*"

"So did everyone else," Mark said. "Twenty years in a wheel chair and she can walk!"

There were fresh blood stains on her dress, at the shoulder, and I became nauseous, thinking that it was Harold's blood until I noticed Mark's hand for the first time. There was a nasty cut on it. "Your hand!" I said. "It's bleeding."

"Nothing serious," Mark said, standing up and facing me for the first time. When he did so, I noticed that his shoulder was bleeding too.

"She stabbed you!" I cried, rushing to him.

"It's nothing," he said, taking me in his arms. "Nothing. Just a flesh wound, that's all."

I was trembling in his arms for fear that he was seriously hurt. "But *you,*" he said. "My God! You've been in this house for days with a mad woman! You could have been killed! It could have been you who was killed," he added, kissing me and hugging me closely.

I couldn't reply. I was too choked up to talk, and weak with relief. The ordeal at Harmer House was over. At the moment I didn't care *why* it had happened, only that it was over for good.

"We've got to get the sheriff out here, and get Edith to the hospital," Mark said.

"What about *your* wounds? Will you be all right until we get to the hospital?"

"Of course, Elizabeth. Really, they're just flesh wounds."

Chapter Fourteen

Edith was still unconscious when we arrived in Mark's car at Blackston Hospital, where she was admitted with a slight concussion and a broken arm.

As Edith and Mark were being examined and treated in the emergency room, one of the hospital personnel called the sheriff. After much confusion (after all, the Harmer case was Blackston's first major crime in thirty-five years and the sheriff and his deputy were indecisive as to how to go about handling the situation), the sheriff finally rode out to Harmer House to investigate and dispatched an ambulance to recover Harold's body.

The sheriff's deputy, a portly, likeable old gentleman with sparse and rumpled hair, early-morning red-rimmed eyes and a night's growth of graying stubble on his face, turned out to be the same man who had taken me to the Kent County Orphanage twenty years earlier.

The revelation was made when he recognized my name while taking my statement. And the next half hour or so, while I waited for Mark to have his wounds attended to, were spent in the deputy's apologizing to me for having had to take me to the orphanage and in my constant assurances that it had all worked out for the best, and that he needn't have regrets for having done his duty.

The apologies and assurances were terminated, finally,

by Mark's emergence from the treatment room, his left hand heavily bandaged.

"That hand looks positively awful!" I said.

Mark laughed. "Just a little cut and a whole pound of bandages," he said. "The doctor says it'll be fine in a week or so."

"What about your shoulder?"

"It's not even as bad as the hand. I was lucky."

The deputy glanced from his clipboard to Mark. "I'm the one that took Miss Gilmore, here, to the orphanage, Mr. Shorewood," he said regretfully.

Mark looked puzzled for a moment, then smiled. "Then she owes you a debt of gratitude," he said.

"Huh?" the deputy said, puzzled.

"Well, thanks to you, she became a big-time New York magazine editor," Mark said. "She never would have had the chance to do so if she hadn't been taken to the orphanage and adopted by the Gilmores."

"Really?" the deputy said, his face alight with relief for the first time.

"Absolutely no doubt about it."

"Well," the deputy said, smiling. "That makes me feel real good! Worst part of my job is taking kids out to that orphanage." He paused, reflecting for a moment. "I've only had to do it three times. Broke my heart everytime. But you know, I'll bet the other two turned out just as well as Miss Gilmore here!"

"I'm sure of it," Mark said.

The deputy brightened, finished taking my statement, then took Mark's, and advised me dutifully and apologetically that I couldn't leave town until after the investigation. "But don't you worry, Miss Gilmore," he said, "we'll get this case straightened out right away. And if you need anything—if there's anything I can do for you while you're in town—you just let me know!"

"I will indeed," I said. "And thank you."

Mark took me in to one of the doctors, who gave me a sedative to counter the effects of shock and to enable me to sleep, then he took me to the Blackston Hotel and registered me. After seeing me to my room and kissing me good night, he left to check on Edith and to see the sheriff, telling me that he'd see me later in the afternoon and would leave word for me at the desk.

I was too exhausted to bathe or eat. It was four a.m. before I finally settled into the comfortable and safe hotel bed behind locked doors, and I fell immediately and soundly to sleep. But sometime—during the hours when I was emerging from deepest sleep, I suppose—I dreamed that I saw the ghost of Angus Harmer again. In my dream, I was sitting at the writing desk in my bedroom at Harmer House and looking down at the paper on which appeared the strange design and the signatures of Julia Carter, when Angus Harmer—kindly and benevolent as I had remembered him from my childhood—entered the room with the sheriff's deputy. Mr. Harmer said nothing, but simply held something out to me. I couldn't distinguish what it was, only that he held it in the palm of his hand, and that it was shiny and flat—like a coin.

The sequence was replaced by a more frightening one. One of Edith in the white bridal gown, the veil pulled back, her expression hideous with hate. She was standing at the front door of Harmer House, and I was standing in the entrance hall beneath the chandelier. The front door was open, and Edith was standing on the threshold, looking at me, her knife raised high above her head, and she was laughing and ringing the front doorbell . . . ringing, ringing. . . .

I was awakened by the ringing. Groggy with sleep and terrified that I had awakened in the house to begin the horrible experience all over again, I sat up, my heart pounding. But I realized that I was safe at the hotel, and the ringing was that of the telephone beside my bed.

I picked up the phone and heard the pleasant voice of the desk clerk, and I remembered that I had left an eleven o'clock call with the desk. The clerk informed me that my car had been brought into town from Harmer House, that my luggage, too, had been brought in and would be sent up in a moment, and that Mark had left word for me to meet him in the lobby at twelve for lunch, if I felt up to it.

After the bellhop brought my luggage up, I took a hot bath, tried in vain to make my hair look presentable, sent a dress downstairs to be pressed, then finally dressed for my luncheon with Mark. All the while, I tried not to think about poor Harold or Edith or Harmer House, but it was simply impossible. And questions were burning in my mind as I descended the carpeted stairs of the old hotel, so preoccupied with my thoughts that it was several seconds before I realized that someone had spoken to me. And I noticed that it was one of the cleaning maids who was just passing me on the stairs. She was looking at me and smiling brightly. "I'm sorry," I said. "I was so preoccupied that I didn't hear you."

"I just said good morning, Miss Gilmore. Did you sleep well?"

"Oh, I certainly did. Thank you."

"I'll be tidying up your room, now, if you're going to be gone for a while."

"Thank you, yes. I'll be gone until later this afternoon, I think."

"Fine," the maid said. "I'm Angela. If you want anything, you just let me know."

"Thank you, Angela, I will. That's very kind of you."

"No trouble, Miss Gilmore," she said, continuing up the stairs. "No trouble at all."

I continued down towards the lobby, thinking how wonderful it was to be alive and among people again.

The lobby smelled of cigar smoke, ancient upholstery and fresh-cut flowers, and it was occupied for the most part by lounging, elderly gentlemen sitting in twos and threes, talking or reading papers or just sitting before the hotel's two large bay windows which looked out onto the activity of Blackston's main street. Outside, it appeared to be warm, and the sun shone brightly.

I had no sooner reached the lobby than the buzzing of conversation stopped, and all eyes followed me across the floor. Even the old gentlemen at the windows turned to stare in my direction. It was suddenly so silent, that only the clicking of my high heels could be heard.

Mark was sitting in a large leather chair near the entrance to the hotel dining room, leafing through a magazine. He looked up when he heard my heels and rose to meet me, smiling.

"You look wonderful!" he said, taking my hand and guiding me towards the dining room. "How on earth can you bounce back from such a nightmare—looking like a dream—with only eight hours' sleep?"

"I think you're using poetic license," I said, laughing.

"Not at all. You're positively beautiful."

"*I* may have bounced back, but I'm afraid my hair didn't," I said, smoothing my hair self-consciously and still looking around the lobby at the myriad of eyes still fixed upon me."

"Nonsense," Mark said. Then, apparently noticing my bewilderment at the attention the people in the lobby were giving me, he added, "You see? Others around here appreciate a beautiful woman when they see one, too."

"Do they always stare at people like that?" I asked as we entered the dining room.

"Sometimes at strangers, yes. But in your case they're impressed. We don't get many celebrities in Blackston, Virginia, you know."

"*Celebrities?*"

"Sure. You've become famous while you were asleep."

"Oh," I said. "No wonder the maid was so concerned about me. So the news is out already."

"Not officially. But this is a small town, and rumors are flying. You're the most celebrated woman in Blackston. I suppose something like this would go almost unnoticed in New York, but here you're definitely front-page news."

Mark continued holding my hand until he helped me with my chair at one of the dining room tables. "I must say," he continued, "this is doing wonders for my ego."

I looked at him quizzically.

Mark smiled. "Yesterday," he said, "I was just another Blackston lawyer. Today, I'm the attorney who knows Elizabeth Gilmore."

"You'd better watch that," I said, kidding him. "They tell me that fame is a fleeting thing."

Mark reached across the table and took my hand. "Not if I keep hanging around the famous Miss Gilmore," he said.

We were interrupted by the waitress who brought us menus. Mark ordered lunch and I ordered breakfast. Mark kept his hand on mine as we sat in silence for a while—the same easy silence I had experienced with him upon our first meeting. I thought about his concern for me when he said that it could have been me who was killed. I thought about his kissing me good night. There was no doubt, from the way he was holding my hand and looking at me, that he was feeling something deeper than friendship for me. I was very flattered and pleased, and the happiest I'd been in months.

The waitress brought our orders, and I began eating immediately. Mark just sat, smiling, watching me.

"I haven't had a thing to eat since we had lunch yesterday," I said.

"It's a wonder you could eat at all in that place, considering all you were going through," he said.

"How's your hand and shoulder? Painful?"

"No, not at all."

"And how's Edith? Have you seen her?"

"Yes," Mark said, starting to eat. "By the way, the editor of the paper would like to take your picture and get a statement from you by three this afternoon, if possible. I told him I might exercise my great influence on you."

"I wouldn't mind," I said. "But what could I tell him? He probably knows more than I do by now. I have more questions than answers."

"I can help you there," Mark said. "The sheriff did a good job of sleuthing while you slept. He told me to tell you that you can leave town whenever you like. The case is closed."

Mark continued eating, and I got the distinct impression that he had no intention of volunteering more information.

"That's all you're going to tell me?" I said.

He shrugged. "I didn't want to upset you by discussing it while you were eating," he said.

"After two nights at Harmer House, *nothing* could upset me. Besides, I've been going crazy with questions since I got up."

Mark smiled. "You're quite a woman, Elizabeth."

"And you're trying to change the subject again," I said, laughing.

"Well, maybe it's because I don't know how to begin apologizing. And I think the story ought to be prefaced by an apology."

"An *apology?* What on earth would you have to apologize about?"

"For even listening to Edith's accusations about you."

I had to laugh. "You saved my life!" I said. "And you've got the scars to prove it! I hardly think an apology's in order."

"You're being kind. And I appreciate it. But if I'd listened to you in the first place . . . well, I should have realized that you wouldn't imagine such things. You really ought to be mad at me—you'd certainly be justified."

"I ought to be mad at you for *thinking* that I could be mad at you," I said. "Edith is a very cunning woman—and most persuasive, too. She even had *me* believing that most of what went on was my imagination! If she could convince *me*, I can hardly blame *you* for believing her. What really puzzles me, is that you changed your mind. I *still* find the whole thing incredible. If I had been you, I don't think I'd ever have believed my crazy story. What made you change your mind? What were you doing at Harmer House so late? It must have been one or two in the morning—I lost all track of time.

"A number of things made me change my mind—too slowly, though, I'm afraid."

"In time enough to save my life," I said. "A couple of minutes later, and—"

"Don't even think about it," Mark interrupted. "Your story about Angus' ghost, the lady in white, the lock missing from your door, the trouble with your car . . . well, it seemed pretty bizarre. . . ."

"It *was* bizarre."

"I know. But your seeming instability just didn't fit you. You struck me as too poised, sophisticated and level-headed for such paranoia. That occurred to me. Then Edith's questioning your sanity before both of us at lunch really stunned me."

"But you must have sensed all that even before you left after lunch yesterday afternoon."

"I did. And it really troubled me. But like I said, it was all so bizarre that I didn't know *what* to think!"

"I had a plan to sneak you into the house after our date, so you could see what was going on for yourself," I said. "I was going to tell you about it at dinner."

"Really?" Mark said. "That's a coincidence. I didn't have any plan in mind, but I wanted to discuss the goings-

132

on at dinner, too. But, of course, when I went to pick you up, Harold told me that you had gone to bed with a bad headache and wouldn't be able to go out with me. So...."

"Then you *did* call for me last night!"

"Sure. About seven."

"I was waiting for you. I heard someone at the door, but Harold told me it was a neighbor."

"That figures. It was all a part of Edith's plan. I kind of wondered about it, but then you had been terribly upset after lunch, and I figured you were probably exhausted.

"Anyway, when Harold told me you were sleeping, I went back into town and had dinner alone at the Regency —that's the restaurant owned by Harold's brother-in-law, Jerred. I talked to Jerred, and I was kidding him, asking how much he had lost to Harold in the poker game Friday night—it was a standing, family joke. Harold was very skilful at poker and was always beating Jerred, and Jerred always claimed that that's why Harold's sister had married him, so Harold could take his money. But Jerred said that Harold didn't play. I told him that I thought Harold had, since he had spent the night, but Jerred said that he had seen Harold only a few minutes when he stopped in the restaurant after picking the car up at the service station. And I remembered that you and Edith both claimed that Harold had stayed in town.

"Jerred said that Harold seemed rather troubled and that he was having problems with Edith. But Harold didn't tell him what kind of problems. I thought the whole thing rather odd, but naturally I didn't realize how serious things were.

"I went to bed, but I slept fitfully, and about one o'clock I woke up and couldn't get back to sleep. I kept thinking about what Jerred had told me and about Edith's comparing you with Julia and about Angus' accidental death. Finally, I got dressed and went out to Harmer House. I figured I'd talk to Harold, and if there was nothing wrong, I'd simply tell him that I was just checking on you, that I was concerned for your health. And that's when I came in."

"But what on earth was it all about?" I asked. "Edith was *walking!* And why did she dress like Julia? Why did she kill Harold? What possible reason could she have had for trying to kill *me?*"

Mark sighed. "That's what we've been unraveling all morning—or trying to," he said, pausing and looking out the dining room window. "You've got a couple of real champions in the sheriff and his deputy. They've really worked hard to get answers for you. But I want you to understand, Elizabeth, that there are certain things about what went on at Harmer House for which there are no answers."

"I don't understand."

"We spent . . . I don't know . . . maybe three hours with Edith today. And the interrogation was as bizarre as the life you lived for the past couple of days. I guess it will come as no surprise to you that Edith is hopelessly insane."

"No," I said. "That certainly doesn't surprise me."

"Well it's worse than you could ever imagine. She readily admits, and without the least remorse, that she killed Harold."

"Because he was going to help me?"

"Yes. But that's not the half of it. Don't feel that she killed because of you. She also confesses to killing Mr. Harmer and Julia as well."

"Oh, no!" I said.

"I'm afraid so. I always wondered about Angus' death, but Julia. . . . After Angus died, there was talk around town about suicide running in the family. You know how that goes. Even I started believing it after a while."

I shuddered. "I can't believe that she'd kill her own daughter and brother!"

"I know. After I saw you to your room, I went back to the hospital and went in with the sheriff to see Edith. When she saw me, they had to tie her down in the bed. She was raging . . . claiming that I had protected Julia, who she said had come back after her."

"*Julia?*"

"Yes. Somehow, in her twisted mind, she thinks that you're Julia—she's convinced of it."

"That explains why she kept calling Julia when I thought the lady in white had her. She was calling to *me!* But how could she possibly think that?"

"I don't know," Mark said, pensively. "One can only guess. You see, you came to Harmer House shortly after Julia's death. Apparently Angus saw a strong resemblance between you and Julia as children. I think that's one of the reasons Angus wanted so badly to adopt you—obviously, he didn't know Edith had killed Julia. And Edith, too, must have sensed something about you that reminded her of Julia. Perhaps there was a resemblance. I don't know."

I tried to visualize the photograph of Julia in her wedding gown. "We were about the same size and build," I said. "But our hair coloring is different, and I don't think there's any facial resemblance."

"I don't know. It was probably just in Edith's crazed mind. There's something else too. I didn't want to tell you, but it does bring some semblance of sense to all this. Angus spoke about you often just before his death. And he planned on insisting upon your coming down to Harmer House for a visit—particularly after he changed his will leaving the place to you. Edith knew he was planning to send for you. And, as you can imagine, if Edith thought of you as Julia, she could hardly be enthusiastic about your return to Harmer House. I suppose, to her, it was like calling the dead back again. She didn't know that Angus had changed his will until after his death. Looking back, now, I can see why it was such a shock to her."

"But why did she kill him?"

"Because in her mind Angus was trying to bring you—Julia—back to Harmer House for revenge. She thought that by killing Angus, you'd have no reason to return. And when she learned that your return was inevitable, she planned to kill you too. Harold had no way of knowing that, of course, and when he turned against Edith to help you, she saw him as one of the conspirators."

"Didn't Harold or Mr. Harmer know that Edith could walk?"

"I don't think anyone did," Mark said. "The sheriff checked her medical records this morning. Edith was afflicted just after Julia's death. The doctor who attended her has since died. But another doctor took over his practice, and his records show that there was no apparent organic cause for Edith's paralysis. Her doctor had diagnosed it as hysteria-induced. I suppose it was because of her guilt. But it's pretty clear now that she feigned paralysis only during the day. With those passageways, it was quite easy for her to lock her bedroom door at night and slip out of the house. Naturally, since it was thought that she was paralyzed, no one suspected that it was she who was seen on the grounds from time to time. It's no wonder Harold was frightened, with her skulking around the grounds at night."

"But why did she kill Julia, do you know?"

"As nearly as we can tell, she was an obsessively possessive woman. I suppose that was one of the manifestations of her insanity. Julia was leaving her to be married. And apparently in Edith's mind, killing Julia kept anyone from taking her daughter from her. According to Jerred, Harold told him that Edith's husband left her when they were living somewhere in Michigan and tried to get custody of Julia through the courts. He must have realized that Edith was insane—or at least had mental problems—even then. Maybe that's why they were separated in the first place. So when Julia's father tried to gain custody of her, Edith brought her back to Blackston to live at Harmer House with Angus. Edith told the sheriff that she fixed it so no one could take Julia away from her, but that she shouldn't have come back."

"That's what she kept saying to me in Julia's room. She kept saying, 'you shouldn't have come back.' "

"She's a very sick woman," Mark said. "Her interrogation was horrifying."

"What will happen to her now? Will she have to stand trial?"

"No. She'd never be sane enough to stand trial. As soon as she recovers from her injuries, she'll be committed."

"Then she really believed that Mr. Harmer had given Harmer House back to her dead daughter to haunt her."

"Yes. Three people dead at the hands of a woman who probably should have been committed twenty years ago."

"And if it hadn't been for you, I'd have been her fourth!" I said, shuddering.

"It's all over now, Elizabeth."

"Except for the estate," I said.

"That's just a matter of signing papers. And that will be over Monday."

"But I don't *want* the estate," I insisted. "I don't want anything to do with it!"

"I think you should reconsider, Elizabeth. Angus wanted you to have it. You can hardly blame him for what Edith did. It was his last wish, you know."

"I know, but right now. . . ."

"Of course," Mark said. "But you know the adage about time healing all wounds. And it's not as though you had to live there. The estate will keep it up."

"I couldn't even bear to look at the place again. I didn't even go out to the old farm where we lived when my father was killed. I couldn't look at it without remembering

137

his death, without seeing him on the ground. It's always the bad things we remember," I said.

Mark reached into his coat pocket. "I nearly forgot this," he said, handing me a white envelope.

"What is it?"

"I don't know. Angus didn't say. He took it from his safe-deposit box at the bank and put it in my safe when he changed his will. My instructions were to give it to you in the event of his death. He said it had once belonged to Julia. He had given it to her."

The envelope was sealed and had my name written across it. I opened it, and a small, thin gold locket fell out. It was inscribed on the back: *to Julia from Uncle Angus*. I turned the locket over and gasped!

"What is it?" Mark said. "What's wrong? You're pale as a ghost!"

I was too stunned to reply. I couldn't take my eyes from the locket. There was a large diamond in the center of it, and around the diamond was engraved the exact, intricate design I had drawn on my stationery my first night at Harmer House, the design I had never seen before!

"What's wrong, Elizabeth?"

I handed Mark the locket and searched through my purse for the crumpled stationery, my hands trembling so badly that I could hardly co-ordinate them.

Mark studied the locket, then looked up at me curiously, unable to see cause for my alarm. I finally found the crumpled paper and handed it to him. He studied the paper for a moment, then looked again at the locket, then up at me, bewildered. "The design is exactly the same!" he said. "Where did you get this paper?"

"It's my stationery," I finally managed to say.

"But how—"

"I don't *know!*" I interrupted. "I just don't know. I drew the design without realizing it when I was writing a letter to occupy my mind the night I saw Mr. Harmer in the library window—Friday night!"

Mark looked to the stationery again, noting the signature. *"Carter!"* he said. "How did you know that name?"

"I don't know *that,* either. I've never known anyone by that name."

"This is astonishing!" Mark commented. "Carter was Julia's father's name. We just learned that today while going over Edith's medical records. You couldn't possibly have known that!"

"That's not all," I said. "Those signatures aren't even in my handwriting. I was writing the letter, and before I knew it, I'd drawn the design and signed the name several times. And, Mark, that design is perfect in every detail. I can't draw that well."

Mark looked at me gravely. "This locket has been in Angus' safe-deposit box for twenty years or so, as far as I know. No one could have reproduced the design from memory except, perhaps . . ."

"Yes?"

"Nothing," he said. "It's not important, now."

"You were going to say, *except Julia,* weren't you?"

"Yes."

We sat looking at one another, silent for a long while, and I recalled with chilling vividness the way my conscious mind seemed to have left me that night as I scrawled the design and signatures in the strange handwriting.

"Mark," I said. "Do you suppose . . ."

Marked looked at me with a quizzical expression, but said nothing.

"Could I have been . . . possessed?" I said.

"By Julia, you mean?"

"Yes. How else could I have known? There's a lot I haven't told you—strange things. Like when Harold was chasing me through the passageways and I found Julia's room. It seemed familiar to me, yet I know I'd never been in there before. Then, while I was looking at her photograph—almost hypnotized by it—I suddenly had a premonition that Edith was going to enter the room. I didn't know that it was Edith at the time, I knew her only as the lady in white, but I *knew* she was going to enter the room. And she did!"

Mark took my hand. "I wish I could console you, somehow," he said. "I wish I had answers to your questions, but I just don't know. There are records of people having been possessed . . . but I don't know, Elizabeth. These are things we'll never know."

"I had a dream this morning, too," I said. "In the dream, Mr. Harmer come to me and offered me *this* locket. I didn't know what it was in the dream, but I do now. And I *did* see him outside the library window that first night. He was standing there, just as I remembered him when I first saw him. And on the service stairs, before you arrived this morning, I thought I saw a glow . . . I don't know, I can't even describe it. I heard a man's voice warning me to leave the house. It wasn't Harold's voice. In my fright, I threw the tea tray I was carrying, and it didn't hit anything! Those stairs are narrow. If someone had been standing on them below me, the tray would have hit him."

Mark studied the locket and my stationery again, shaking his head in dismay, then handed them back to me. "What can I say?"

"You *do* believe me, don't you, Mark?"

He motioned for the waitress and paid the check. "Of course I believe you," he said. "Look, let's get out of here. How about a walk in the sunshine and fresh air? It'll make you feel like a new woman. I'll even show you the town—all three blocks of it," he promised, smiling.

We crossed the lobby under the watchful eyes of the loungers. Some of them nodded or waved as we left the hotel and walked along the main street, passing the hotel's large bay windows. Mark held my hand as we walked.

"I've been thinking about your conversation with the deputy this morning—about his taking me to the orphanage," I said.

"Oh? What were you thinking?"

"I was really bothered by his guilt. He really felt badly about taking me from Harmer House."

"Yes, I noticed."

"That was a nice thing you told him. You're a very kind man, Mr. Shorewood."

"I thought you'd never notice," Mark said, smiling.

"One couldn't help noticing."

"Is that a proposal, Miss Gilmore?"

I must have worn a sorrowful expression, for despite Mark's light-hearted remark, I was still lost in my haunted memories, and I fell silent. But Mark began directing my attention to shop windows and making humorous remarks in an obvious effort to take my mind off my dark thoughts. "Hey, how about a new hat?" he said.

"A new *hat?*" I echoed, distracted.

"Sure. I've heard all about you women—how there's nothing like a new hat to raise your spirits. Do you realize that in the three days and two nights I've known you, I've never bought you a new hat?"

I smiled. "I really don't care for one. I seldom wear hats."

He pulled me to an abrupt stop before a hardware store, peering into the window. "All right, then," he said. "How about a gallon of paint—any color, you name it."

I had to laugh. "No. I think not," I said.

"Hmm. Hard to please, huh? You're certainly hard to buy a gift for. How about a shovel, then? Look at that, they've got this terrific special on shovels."

"Mark! Be serious," I pleaded. "What am I going to do?"

141

"Smile," he said. "Smile and forget the past. That's all you *can* do. It's all over, Elizabeth, don't you understand that?"

"I wish it were that easy."

"It is."

"But. . . ."

"Are you seriously trying to out-argue a lawyer?" Mark interrupted. "Everybody knows you can't out-argue a lawyer. Listen, you were an English major, weren't you?"

"An English major? Yes, why?"

"Didn't you ever read T.S. Eliot?"

"Yes."

"Don't you remember when he said that man cannot stand too much reality?"

"Yes, I think so."

"Well, that goes for *supernatural* reality too. You're *here*, Elizabeth. Now. Safe. And best of all, you're with *me!* Now that ought to be worth something! Not everybody can be with *me*, you know," he said, striking a pose in mock pride.

"You've got a point, there," I said.

"And another thing," Mark said, taking my hand again and literally pulling me along. "Did you, or did you not, weasel out of a dinner date with me? Careful now, you're under oath!"

"I can't deny it, but there were extenuating circumstances."

"Overruled. I demand a rematch."

"I'd be delighted."

"Tonight."

"How can I refuse? One can't argue with a lawyer."

"But there are strings attached, of course."

"Oh?"

"Yes. You've just made a commitment, and that's a verbal contract. There's fine print, too. We lawyers revel in fine print, you know."